I0529880

Lillian Holmes and the Leaping Man

Ciar Cullen

"Smart, funny, exciting…Ms. Cullen provides endearing characters, a unique premise, and a very satisfying resolution. I not only couldn't put it down, but I'll recommend it to my friends." —*New York Times* Bestselling Author Susan Squires

"Sherlock Holmes would be proud to have such a relation. *The Leaping Man* will take its place in the annals of romantic vampire lore." —Melanie Jackson, Bestselling Author of the Chloe Boston Mysteries

THE LEAPING MAN

It was not relief Lillian found. Through the fine mist that diffused the lights on the empty street below she peered. There beneath her, at first unaware of her detection, a man had dropped from a neighboring balcony two stories above. When he hit the ground with the grace of a feline, he turned and glanced up as if he'd felt her stare.

A chill ran through Lillian's bones at that glance, at the sight of a man who should have broken limbs and bruises if he survived the fall at all. Still, he was most certainly a man, and a cheeky one at that. Lillian brought her arms across her chest at his intense gaze. Knowing she should shift, that she should hide her nudity from a stranger, she tried to inch back but still keep sight of him. Her feet would barely move.

In the darkness, before he slipped into the black shadows, he smiled and tipped his cap, chuckling as he disappeared.

Lillian Holmes and the Leaping Man

Ciar Cullen

4

www.BOROUGHSPUBLISHINGGROUP.com

LILLIAN HOLMES AND THE LEAPING MAN
Copyright © 2015 Ciar Cullen

ISBN 978-1-942886-42-6

For Lil Twamley, born 1890. My muse, grandmother and dearest childhood friend.

ACKNOWLEDGMENTS

For unwavering encouragement, I owe a great debt to my husband. For constantly asking "Where's that Holmes story?" I thank my beloved late brother, Tom. For accepting a sow's ear and helping to patch it into some kind of usable purse, I am greatly indebted to the exceptionally talented Chris Keeslar. Anne Cain, thank you for another fantastic cover.

CONTENTS

CHAPTER ONE

In which our heroine's first case presents itself.

Baltimore, 1899

Lillian Holmes strapped on goggles and shoved her long black hair under her leather cap. She wanted to go fast on a day that always made her feel jittery.

It wasn't logical that she should feel much of anything, she reminded herself, for facts were facts and knowledge was always good. Except that on this day seventeen years earlier, at age seven, perhaps she hadn't been ready for facts. At least not ones so stark and final:

Mother had died in childbirth.

Father was never coming home, perished with the *SS Gothenburg* off Australia in 1875.

She'd stopped listening that day, the room blurring and buzzing as blood pounded in her ears and pain poured out in quiet tears. Of course she'd known already that she was an orphan, but questions burgeoned as she grew older, and evidently the adults in her life felt it time to tell her the truth. August 28, 1883. Lillian remembered the date because she'd stared at the newspaper thrown on the green brocade settee as her governess told her the story. The headline spoke of France, of looming war, and of the eruption of a volcano on an exotic island named Krakatau—all far away things, like Addie's kind voice as it faded into the background.

In the following seventeen years, Lillian never asked her governess for details. The unasked questions still lay buried like ancient treasures beneath the walls she'd built around herself. Do I have grandparents or siblings, Addie? Why was Father on a ship so far away when his wife was with child? Why am I wealthy? Did you know my mother? Do I look like her?

On this, the sixteenth anniversary of the Truth of Lillian Holmes as she'd titled the day in her journal, Lillian slung her leather satchel over her shoulder. It held her most prized possessions: her Journal of Important Observations, two novels, one in French, one letter, and the Colt revolver she'd bought for herself on her twenty-first birthday. She was prepared for adventure.

In the lingering late August heat wave, her neighbors would have their windows flung wide and might hear the engine of her steam-powered velocipede. Well, the vehicle technically belonged to her butler, Thomas, but he let Lillian ride it now and then. Thomas hated that she rode at night, but he knew that she couldn't afford to be seen at such an unseemly pastime. No, the neighbors would talk, the talk would spread, and Lillian would be back in the clutches of the men who watched her like a hawk: her solicitor and her physician. Suddenly angry at the thought of her lack of control over her own life, Lillian determined to ride far tonight. Her neighbors would not recognize her in any case: her boy's trousers and loose shirt would hide her form.

It was the beginning of dead time, as she'd come to think of the hours between midnight and three, when insanity or some innate evil drove her fellow mortals to unthinkable acts, including the recent foul murder of Baltimore's mayor only blocks away. But Lillian didn't fear the night. She could outrun the shadows and outwit any enemy.

So dramatic, Lillian. As if you actually have an enemy.

Still, she thought it would be good fun to have a nemesis, like Uncle had the evil Professor Moriarity. While her closest friend— nay, her only friend—Bess, might think that forces of an otherworldly nature worked evil upon the good citizens of Baltimore, Lillian cared only about facts. *"Give me data!"* Uncle Sherlock's mantra pulled her to reason whenever Bess tried to lure her to fanciful musings. And whenever the Melancholies came calling—and they usually did so late at night—she'd immerse herself in the fading memories of her single year in London with Uncle.

A nemesis would come in right handy to prove her brilliance. The closest she had was a loathsome greedy solicitor who seemed to delight in her troubles.

Troubles. No, she was overcoming her troubles, she'd assured Dr. Schneider, and would continue to improve. It was a passing thing, these sad spells, and a fast ride was good medicine.

"He is not my real uncle; he is not real at all," Lillian said aloud to no one, a practiced phrase she'd sworn to repeat whenever her fantasy took hold. Dr. Schneider had taken great pains to explain, more than once, that if Lillian could not rid herself of this "most extraordinary delusion," he would recommend further treatment. Lillian shuddered at the thought of what that treatment might entail—a stay at Spring Grove for lunacy, a drill through the skull?

"I was never in London. He is not my real uncle," she repeated.

Her solicitor, Francis Pemberton, had made it quite clear that two things hung on her ability to be a normal lady of society: her fortune and her freedom. She cared much more about the latter, knowing that the odious man would like nothing more than to see her rot in an asylum. How he would claim her fortune for himself she wasn't sure, but that he would attempt to rob her one day she was certain.

No, she vowed. He would not win. At least she could pretend to be a normal lady.

Bess would help. She *must* help. Bess had helped so often, offering excuses to acquaintances when Lillian's Melancholies gripped her tightly, escorting Lillian to essential events for a lady to attend, although she hadn't the least bit of interest in them. Bess was two years younger than Lillian, at 22, but she schooled her in all manner of topics Lillian cared not about: frocks and hats, gloves and dancing, fans and flirting.

Lillian walked the velocipede across the street. As she did, she gazed down toward the harbor at Federal Hill, which seemed to guard the good citizens of Baltimore from any outside evil, as it had done when the Country was born. With each step she rehearsed Uncle's words—

Words penned by Mister Conan Doyle, she quickly corrected herself. *No act goes without leaving a trace, no criminal is brilliant enough to evade scientific inquiry, and no task is too arduous for one who puts aside emotion for reason.* Of course, Uncle Sherlock would not approve of how frivolously she had spent her day, taking a lesson on popular songs from Bess, but no one would approve of how she meant to spend the night. She would ride, and not even Bess's imaginary phantoms would be able to keep up.

The path Lillian chose wound down from a deserted Light Street, past shops and ships, streetlamps, some electric and some fueled with oil. The lights diminished as she ventured away from the city center to distant Druid Hill Park where paths scarred the manicured landscape like rivulets of blackening blood leading into forbidden darkness. It mattered not who lurked there, she reminded herself as she leaned forward, a push of the pedal and a flick of a switch igniting the spark to let her fly; this was her secret world where darkness promised freedom, where solitude allowed her the luxury of not standing out as a "most unusual girl." Pemberton would not see. No one would see.

Lillian wound past the Great Lake, and as was her custom she stopped to climb the steep retaining wall and take in the solitude and the moonlight's still reflection on the shimmering water, turned as if by alchemy into mercury. Tonight, she lingered. Lillian pulled off her goggles and angled the letter she pulled from her pants pocket to catch the light on it. Worn from too much folding and unfolding, and in truth stained from a few tears, she reread the treasure.

Dear Miss Holmes,

Thank you for your kind letter regarding my Sherlock Holmes stories. I never imagined my tales would catch the interest of readers across the Atlantic in such quick measure.

I regret to say that while my character is loosely based on an acquaintance, the name Holmes is a choice made by me, the novelist, and carries no significance. I am afraid I am unable to help you locate your ancestors.

I believe by the tone of your inquiry that this information might bring you great sadness. In recent months I have begun a serious study of Spiritism, and while you may not understand the field that is considered quite fantastical by most, it has influenced my opinions on the nature of this mortal realm. It is my humble opinion that destiny is not predetermined by heritage, but by forces we cannot clearly imagine. One must follow an inner calling if one is fortunate enough to be called. If you desire to be like my Holmes and become the first female detective in America, there is little to stop you, is there not?

One note of warning. Please take great care in your investigations. There is true evil in this world, far more evil than I have penned in my tales—because it is not fictional. Do not put yourself in harm's way.

Sherlock, Mycroft and Doctor Watson send their warm regards, as do I.

Yours,
Arthur C. Doyle

Lillian folded the treasure with reverence and closed her eyes to bring forth a favored fantasy. Uncle Sherlock sat in his favorite chair, smoke curling from his pipe, attending to her every word while pretending absorption in a book on his lap. Dr. Watson bustled about their quarters looking for some misplaced item, muttering that the housekeeper moved it.

Uncle listened, truly listened, as if her words mattered. As if *she* mattered. Lillian knew now how silly she must have sounded as she expounded on her theory of a sensational London murder, but Uncle closed his book and stared at her intently. She fell mute, embarrassed, ready to be corrected. He raised one brow and took a long draw on his pipe. His fine features, so unlike his brother Mycroft's but so like her own, seemed sharper in the dark light of the cozy parlor.

Just when she thought the subject was closed, he spoke. "Lillian, I believe you may one day prove to have the finest mind I've encountered among your sex. What do you say, Watson?"

"What's that, Holmes? Oh, of course she's brilliant. And quite lovely."

"Yes, lovely. Her mother was lovely as well." And Uncle was lost in thought again, but his words lingered. She was brilliant. Or would be.

Lillian pushed the letter back into her pocket and mounted her transport, resolving anew to solve a criminal mystery before the first leaves of autumn hit the earth. She imagined the triumphant letter she would send to Uncle Sherlock, and how Dr. Schneider and Mr. Pemberton would feel chagrined.

No, she corrected. She would write *Mister Conan Doyle*, and he would perhaps include her tale in one of his stories. In that way, she would be *as* a niece of Sherlock Holmes.

Her spirits lifted, she took a complete spin around the park, pulling her cap off and letting her long hair fly free and whip about her face. She leaned into the curve, excitement bubbling up as she kept her balance on the muddy gutters.

Faster still! Was that her voice? She'd heard it on the breeze, she was sure. A boy sitting on the curb jumped to his feet as she approached to avoid disaster, but he waved his cap in the air and hooted in appreciation, and perhaps jealousy, as she left him far behind.

She sped back down the gentle slope that drew her to the harbor, back to her home, past a few hansom cabs returning members of society from dreary dinners and concerts. Like the dreams she had as a child of flying along a beach, like sailing on a fast schooner, ducking this way and that with a change of the angle of her arms... Her speed made her thoughts slow and her heart calm.

The city rose to meet her, buildings looming above. She rode past the Mt. Vernon monument, glancing up at the immense marble statue, sorry to be again within the surrounding cave of stone buildings. Secrets still beckoned. *Don't go home,* the statue of George Washington whispered over distant clip-clop of hooves and squealing metal trolley wheels that slowed on their rails. Lillian wound around cabs and carts, but the city was relentless, as if it intended to pull her down the length of the harbor, past the maze of slums and factories, right to the great shipping docks and into the bay.

"No!" she argued. "Not tonight."

There is so much to see. So much to learn. We will wait for you, the city whispered for her alone.

"Hush! You are not to speak to me!"

The pain would end, deep in the harbor, dark and quiet...

"Silence!"

A police whistle set her nerves sizzling and she rounded Federal Hill at a reckless speed, hoping the constable was on foot rather than horseback. She didn't turn to see, but lay low and clutched the motorcycle handles for dear life. What would Thomas say if he had to come so far to collect her from a prison?

The streetlight nearest her house had never sent relief rushing through her before, the prospect of her bed never so welcoming. How long had she ridden? It had seemed like a moment rather than an hour.

She cut the engine and walked the vehicle down the dirt alley to her gardener's shed. At the snap of a twig, she jumped and spun to face the towering figure of her butler. He rubbed at his chin and narrowed his eyes.

"G'evening, Miss. Or should I say good day to you, as it is past midnight?"

"Hello will do, Thomas. So, you heard me leave. I must oil the lock on the shed. You did not need to wait up for me."

He scolded her with an arch of his brow. That brow had brought a flush of shame to Lillian's cheeks many times through the years. Thomas Adencourt, her governess's older brother, walked with a decided limp, a painful reminder of his time in Union blue at Andersonville prison. The miracle of keeping his leg when so many had lost a limb to a Confederate shot was also his curse. He'd often threaten to cut the painful flesh and bone away himself.

While he tried to hide it from her, she could see he was in agony this night. Lillian didn't doubt he would douse that hurt with a good swig of whiskey before retiring. She wondered if he'd managed to douse the mental hurt of the war that had taken both his brothers.

"As you can see, I have returned your machine without a nick of the frame or mud upon the wheels." She glanced down and wiped away some mud with her leather glove. "Perhaps a bit of mud. I shall remedy that."

"I see you collected the mud on your face as well." Thomas sighed and gave her a friendly nudge towards the house. "You'll be the death of me. Nothing gets by Mrs. Adencourt. When she worries about you, she takes it out on me."

"Addie chooses her battles wisely, Thomas. Don't fret so. Now show me some of your latest contraptions. I'd like to see how you're getting on with that small spyglass I fancy…"

"Time for sleep, Miss Holmes! Dr. Schneider said sleep is essential to your health. And the Lord knows it's essential to this old body."

"Dr. Schneider would have me sleep my life away." *And how nice that sounds right now.*

"You must be careful, Lillian. Addie frets constantly about you. Take care, my dear. A little ride now and then…well, that can stay between us. Be temperate, girl. At least, be outwardly temperate. Did you take your pistol?"

"Of course."

Thomas nodded and let out a deep breath, and Lillian cursed herself. The butler looked quite exhausted. She'd taken advantage of the wide berth he'd allowed her all these years.

"Thomas," she whispered to stop him in his tracks.

He turned. "Yes, Miss?"

"I thank you much for all you do for me. I mean, that you allow me to…to be me. That you trust me." *If I needed a father, I would want him to be you.*

A fleeting smile disappeared so quickly Lillian thought she imagined it. Then Thomas nodded and mumbled something as he opened the rear door to the house.

When alone in her room, Lillian stepped out of her clothes, washed her face, and retrieved the bottle of Mrs. Winslow's remedy from its hiding place. She pushed down Dr. Schneider's severe scolding about her habit and took a deep swig from the bottle. She'd argued that mothers gave teething babies a dose of the liquid, so it could not be strong. He'd cursed in German and added, "You can quiet an infant into the grave, Lillian. You can quiet your own cries the same way."

Next week, I will give it up next week. Only on this anniversary. To sleep.

Her nerves calmed, she fell asleep quickly—only to awaken in a sweat an hour later. She tossed and turned in the stifling heat and finally discarded her clinging nightclothes to a heap on the bed and approached the window for some relief.

It was not relief she found. Through the fine mist that diffused the lights on the empty street below Lillian peered. There beneath her, at first unaware of her detection, a man had dropped from a neighboring balcony two stories above. When he hit the ground with the grace of a feline, he turned and glanced up as if he'd felt her stare.

A chill ran through Lillian's bones at that glance, at the sight of a man who should have broken limbs and bruises if he survived the fall at all. Still, he was most certainly a man, and a cheeky one at that. Lillian brought her arms across her chest at his intense gaze. Knowing she should shift, that she should hide her nudity from a stranger, she tried to inch back but still keep sight of him. Her feet would barely move.

In the darkness, before he slipped into the black shadows, he smiled and tipped his cap, chuckling as he disappeared.

Lillian assumed her neighbor had taken a lover, as gossipers reported such was the widow's unseemly habit, and put the incident aside as a rather uninteresting example of human frailty. She took the time, however, to flatten a new page in her Journal of Observations, and to make an accurate notation of the event. She noted the man's tall stature, his lean look, the angularity of his features, the deepness of his eyes and the paleness of his skin—or had that been a function of the streetlight and shadows? And yes, she added as an afterthought, his face was splendid. Perfect, in fact.

The image of the Leaping Man burned in her brain until she fell into a fitful nightmare of her departed mother reaching out to her and whispering silent endearments. Yes, the Melancholies always came on August 28th .

***

The hue and cry in the morning proved Lillian's first hypothesis about the Leaping Man wrong, and she reprimanded herself for the error. This had nothing to do with the appetites of the widow Mrs. Gilvarg. Paul Stephenson, the youngest of a family of five that had moved into the house two doors down, was dead of an apparent suicide, all the blood having seeped from a series of gashes to his neck. He'd dropped the knife on the floor near his bed.

"Surely the detectives see the similarity to the murder of Mayor Blackstone!" she cried at breakfast. "This young man did not take his own life!"

Thomas shook his head, and without looking up from his cup of tea he grumbled, "Leave it be, Lillian."

She must go to the authorities at once.

I saw him. He smiled at me. Her stomach churned, and blood turned to ice in her veins. A craving for a soothing bit of tonic made her hands shake.

"Addie, Thomas, please listen to me. I saw the murderer. He wore a dark fisherman's cap. Tall, very tall, and broad shouldered. He jumped from a two-story balcony and landed like a cat, sure-footed and calm, however improbable that seems. *I saw him.*"

"Oh, Lil." Addie looked up from her needlework and sighed. "You promised you would at least *try*. Shall I call the Doctor?"

"I would take an oath on Uncle's..." *You have no uncle. How could you be so stupid? Now they will never believe you.*

"This is most upsetting to us all, Lil. Retire to your room and rest. I'll be up with a fresh pot of tea, how will that be?"

Addie shared a quick look with her brother, and Lillian knew all was lost. If the two people who loved her most didn't believe her, the authorities would surely not. They would send for Dr. Schneider that very day.

Well, then, it will be my case, my secret. Uncle would keep the clues to himself until he could fully solve them, and once all was clear, he'd report his dramatic findings to Scotland Yard. Lillian would do the same, and she looked forward to the spectacle she would create, the headlines and accolades.

Oh, what a letter she would write, she swore as she closed her door and reached for her bottle of Mrs. Winslow's.

CHAPTER TWO

An irrepressible fugitive returns.

George rose from bed, having slept soundly through the day, sated with the blood of a healthy young man, his favorite meal. He stuffed his bloodied cap and jacket into the fireplace, rolled up the newsprint strewn about the floor, lit a match and threw it in after them, congratulating himself for remembering to secure a room at the Altamont Hotel with a fireplace. They often came in handy, even in the stifling heat of late summer.

While the place wasn't particularly up to his standards and he preferred the clientele of the Rennard, his room offered an unobstructed view of the elegant homes on Eutaw Street. So irritating, this confinement. As far as everyone knew, including his brother Phillip, he was across the seas, whiling away fifty years or so. But in less than a year, his enemies, and they were now numerous, had forced his retreat back to Baltimore.

How had Marie de Bourbon done it? In the decade he and his brother were in America, she'd managed a total coup of the French and British Houses: two hundred vampyre, at least, under her control, including his own mother. Those who fought her were perished or scattered across the continent. Madam Lucifer had once again earned her name. And now, rumors among the House in New York hinted she had set her sights on America.

Of course, the sighting in New Orleans of a woman fitting her description was likely nothing. The voodoo priestesses of that city had invented all manner of creature, including the phantom

22

Loogarou. Vampire-wolves, indeed. He snorted. It was a city of hysteria.

George wished Marie *would* go to New Orleans. She'd have some competition there, as well as some capable human adversaries from Africa and the Caribbean. How could he amass comrades in this pitiful city? Besides a few fledglings he'd only recently kicked from the nest, there was only one with any power at all, only one other of his kind he could count on: his brother. No, it would take decades to build a House of any size at all. Trustworthy children, with fealty to him and his favorites alone, built strong by the maker's bond, and enriched by many "grandchildren" and "great-grandchildren." Neither George nor Phillip had ever had a taste for the politics of vampire regimes, choosing instead to live more solitary lives in less attractive cities. Like this one.

But now, without such a following, those who had lived such solitary lives were at extreme risk, as Houses grew in numbers and powers, spreading quickly through America and God knew where else. And George, perhaps, was at the greatest risk of all, having brushed up against a Queen with a voracious appetite and taste for power and revenge.

"Won't Phillip be surprised," George whispered to the hissing fireplace.

And, *Won't he hate you for breaking your agreement? Won't he try to kill you to protect his lovely new bride?* His brother would die in any such attempt to destroy his maker, but he would likely sacrifice himself nonetheless. Phillip tended toward heroics. They were as night and day. For as sure as the sun would set in a few moments, George knew that Phillip had allowed his sweet little Kitty Twamley to remain human, flesh and untainted blood, while he feasted alone on the criminal element of Baltimore.

So noble, so naïve, George thought as he pulled on his pipe. When the pretty lass started to age, when her flesh sagged and wrinkled, Phillip would regret his decision. How many mortal women had they buried through the centuries? How many had they left to rot where they lay? How many had they brought into the fold? They should have kept a journal, he mused.

George watched the last finger of light shorten its reach on the carpet and recede into twilight; then he pulled the heavy curtain back a fraction to ensure darkness had indeed fallen and it was safe to draw wider so he could spy on his neighbors. While Phillip seemed to take after their mother and was unaffected by daylight, George, like most of their kind, grew weak with extended exposure to the sun.

Three days, and no sign of Phillip or Kitty. He'd seen familiar figures enough: the tiresome Langhan sisters on some social jaunt each evening. The fruit vendor—hadn't he done in his brother? Or was that the butcher? The city's slow-witted policemen didn't have time or inclination to solve the murders of the lower classes, and George snickered. They were still licking their wounds after allowing the mayor's murder. Or, as most still believed, suicide.

Where is *he?* It wouldn't do for his enemy or one of her lieutenants to find him before he had a chance to elicit allegiance from Phillip.

Had the pair married already and honeymooned abroad? Subtle inquiries suggested Phillip still resided in the mansion he and George shared before Kitty stumbled into their lives. Perhaps his brother was avoiding him, having tasted a year free of the bond of his maker. Or, emotional chap that he was, perhaps he'd actually missed George. George would have to ascertain which, quickly, to know how to play best on Phillip's intense romanticism.

George's attention was drawn to a tall, slender, raven-haired woman who emerged from a house a few doors down the street. Her carriage was striking, her figure curvaceous enough to bring his lust to life. How old was she? He imagined her twenties, given her simple but stylish dress. Her face shielded a bit by her wide hat, she fretted with her gloves and bag and stopped for a moment.

Why so nervous, lovely lady? Did she step out to meet a lover?

A pack of little ruffians, none older than twelve or so, materialized as if from thin air and circled her, giggling and pulling at her hand.

"She'll be robbed, stupid girl!" He laughed at the simple tricks of the rapscallions. He'd separated enough women from their jewels and purses as a youth, using his charm and captivating mortal good looks.

But no, she laughed with them and scooped the youngest up into her arms. One held an oversized hound by a rope, although the dog seemed to be leading the boy.

George shrugged and turned away. Another insipid girl in an uninteresting century, in a most uninteresting city. But as she turned to speak to the children, he caught a glimpse of her face and froze. The woman from last night! Hadn't she looked quite different with the moonlight shining on her long silky hair, her arms barely concealing her breasts, her gently rounded hips visible above that window ledge? What had she thought, seeing him jump two stories to the street? She must have believed she was dreaming. Had he not been in a euphoric state from the blood of the young chap he'd devoured, he'd likely have taken her too.

George smiled, making a mental note of a potentially enjoyable meal. Didn't she know the streets were not safe at night?

He brushed his hands over his face, thinking for a moment of the days when a beautiful woman was a different kind of meal, quenched a different thirst. He would murder, but he wasn't a rapist, and he didn't have time or interest in courting such a lady of society. God, but this era was tiresome, with table legs wrapped in cloth against impropriety. Peeling the layers of clothing off a woman like that would take weeks, possibly months… No, he'd have to settle with the whores of Fell's Point.

He jumped at the knock on his door, and as he approached it, he sensed that his brother had found him first. And he felt Phillip's anger.

"It's all right, Georgy, let me in," his brother called.

George drew his power up in a breath and opened the door, then nonchalantly turned his back on his sibling and retrieved his pipe. He stared out the window, waiting for Phillip to speak first, but the room remained silent. Finally he turned, finding the eyes of the first person he'd made immortal. His only ally, willing or not.

"I despise you for making me hide out in this dreadful place. Where have you been?"

"You said you'd stay away until Kitty's natural life came to an end. You promised, George. Of course, I am once again the fool for believing you."

"Yes, I love you too. Now, where have you been?"

"What does it matter?"

George tilted his head and sent the force of his will into Phillip's chest. Yes, the connection remained.

"New Orleans, damn you to hell."

"Too much competition in that city."

"We were there so Kitty could paint a portrait. A handsome commission, too. I care not about the New Orleans House. A more pompous, egotistical society I never encountered. You would fit in nicely."

"And does our long-lost cousin still run that House? Do we still find favor among his brood? I recall he made you a handsome offer some decades ago?"

"Looking for a post are you, George? You want to be Jean's errand-boy? I find that quite amusing."

"I simply like to keep up on the latest comings and goings."

"I felt you as soon as I returned." His brother shook his head morosely and sat. "I thought our bond fully broken when you left for London."

"You thought you'd be completely free of me—at least for many years." George had expected his brother's disappointment, but not that it would hurt his pride. "The maker bond is as strong as ever, isn't it? I feel it to be so."

"And now you will strengthen it, and I'll be at your mercy again. Sadly enough, part of me welcomes it. I'm so used to fighting you at every turn, trying to undo the havoc you wreak; I've barely known what to do with myself with all my free time."

"Sarcasm is not your strong point."

"At least now I'll have you to blame for all of my own mistakes as well." Phillip loosened his cravat and leaned back into the cushions.

"Like Kitty?" George held his hand up to ward off the coming attack. "Ah, old habits die hard. Kitty is not a mistake in your eyes. But I know the temptation to take her blood must be overwhelming at times. How does she fare?"

"She is well, as if you care. But you are not here for her, so tell me what brings you back. We had a bargain."

"I don't mind Kitty that much. Although she might be in the way now."

"*You* are in the way. She is to be my wife."

George paced in front of the fireplace, now only embers. "Madam Lucifer is at it again. Marie de Bourbon is unalive, well, and on a new crusade against me."

Phillip laughed. "Oh, bloody hell, George. Is that all? My ex-wife threatened you? Did you call her portly again?"

"It's not funny. She has a long memory."

"Yes, well, it's a little hard to forget that your brother-in-law turned your husband into a vampire. She was somewhat fond of me.

At least, I think she was. Didn't like either of us much after you drained her, too."

"I was a bit relentless in those first weeks."

"You were quite insane, as I've not seen since in any House. You killed for sport, it seemed."

George spun away from Phillip and rubbed at his chin. *Don't lose your temper just yet. Let him get a few digs in.* "I concur. It was not my finest moment. In any case, I released Marie's bond centuries ago in a moment of weakness. I should have killed her when I had the chance."

"So kill her now, what do I care? She's loathsome and would certainly take me down with you, along with my Kitty. You'd be doing us all a favor. What can I do about any of this? If she's too strong for you, then she's far too strong for me."

George spun on his heel to face his brother. *Don't scare him away.* "She's amassed an enormous following, Phillip. If I stepped foot in France or England, her Houses would be on me in an instant. It was dreadful in London. You've been away too long. It's a veritable war. Her, Mother—"

"Mother? You saw her?"

That was a low blow, George admitted, but it was the one card he had up his sleeve. Phillip always softened at the mention of her. Their mother had wanted little to do with George since in a moment of weakness he'd become his brother's maker. Still, she had little room to talk, didn't she? George himself had been *her* first meal.

"She can take care of herself. But she won't help me, and we both know why. So Madam Lucifer continues her hunt unimpeded. I have no allies. Evidently I do not inspire devotion. I cannot imagine why."

He sniffed out a laugh, but Phillip remained stone-faced. "Why hide here? Go to some exotic outpost, to the Orient or the western frontier of America! Why involve me in your mess?"

George turned away. So, there it was. He would have to use force. Phillip would cover the same familiar ground, and how could George blame him? He'd destroyed his brother's soul in one frenzied moment of hunger, need, and loneliness. His first taste of mortal blood.

"Marie may listen to you. I'm sure there's some affection left in those icy veins. You are the father of her child. We think. Tell her, Phillip, ask her, beg her to let us stay in the dark alleyways of small unappealing towns. Tell her we are no threat."

"If she has amassed the following you claim, you do indeed pose no threat. She was strong from the first day. Do you suspect her of attacking her own children?"

"There can be no doubt of it! She rules through fear. You must try to dissuade her, plea on my behalf, tell her that we are at peace!"

"Are we at peace, George? Truly? Now that you are in Baltimore, I must look over my shoulder constantly, wondering who you will strike next. I come home from New Orleans to learn my young neighbor died of an apparent suicide. The *mayor* also died of his own hand a few days before that, knife drawn across his throat and then cast aside in the same manner. Does no one own a pistol in this town? Baltimoreans evidently choose to slice their own throats when they can no longer stand to live. Can I expect my beautiful fiancée to slit her throat if I should go away for a night? The law might not have made the connection, but I certainly saw your modus operandi in those deaths. How are we at peace when I cannot trust you to be in the same city as my beloved?"

"You can trust me not to harm Kitty. Of course you can. I cannot undo what has been done, brother. I cannot give your short human life back, your funeral procession, and a grave in Saint-Denis. Don't you think I've lived with regret?" George smelled the guilt wafting from Phillip. This tactic had always worked, and it would work now. "It is the one true shame of my life."

Phillip held up his hand for silence. "I am sorry. I promised myself years ago not to lord it over you. I know your regret. We were young and you were weak and nearly insane with isolation, with betrayal over mother's act. It was your way of hurting her; we both know that. But what of our bargain? What am I to do now? You would bring a vampire-eater down on me as well?"

He pushed his hand through his hair and paced the length of the room. "Kitty will turn you in if you continue to slaughter innocents. Her moral compass shows one direction only—goodness. She gives me leeway, as you know, only because I hunt the already damned. If you see her as a threat, you will kill her, I know it. Your loyalty to me does not outweigh your wanton desires. What would you have me do, George!"

"I've had time to think this through. I have weighed everything. I know Kitty loathes me. If I could change her mind, would you then help me?"

"Change her mind? Not a chance of it."

"If I were to become like the man she loves, how could she not love me? If I were to haunt the docks and alleys, feasting only on criminals or their victims? What would she think then?"

"You could not do it, would not even try. This is a trick, and not so clever a one that she won't see through it as well."

"I can, and I will. If you swear you will help should Marie track me down, to help me gather allies in this godforsaken region of this godforsaken country, I will swear to be an upstanding citizen of this fair city."

"Ridiculous."

"Give me one week, Phillip. You will see." But his plea came with a dose of command, and he saw his brother grimace with pain.

"How will I convince her? God, you are so frustrating!"

"Splendid!" George nodded at his sibling's acquiescence. "You won't need to convince her, she'll see for herself. Do tell her I'm about, though, darling. Don't want to scare her to death."

"If you make one false move, George, one hint of a false move, I will not hesitate to help Madam Lucifer take you down. Am I clear?"

"Nonsense. You wouldn't know how to begin."

"But Marie de Bourbon would."

"Touché. So, when will you get me out of this damned hotel? I would have my old rooms back."

"You are truly delusional."

"By Saturday?"

"Let me talk to Kitty first. She still lives with the Langhan sisters. We are to be married at Christmas, so you must be out by then. Unless of course I kill you first."

"But you won't. Do you know why, brother?"

When Phillip shook his head, George just waved him on his way. It was too painful to speak aloud.

He feels sorry for me. I used to rule the world, and now I have to use my control to gain his assistance. It was his brother's weakness, this sympathy for him.

"So, there is something worse than being loathed," he whispered to the last wink of fireplace embers.

CHAPTER THREE

Shallow men and handsome rakes.

Lillian fussed with her mother's amethyst ring, the lone piece of jewelry she wore, struggling not to appear annoyed. The earnest and handsome suitor currently wasting her precious time made her skin crawl.

Part of her unwritten contract with Addie was that she would accept visitors, one a month. When she was younger, Lillian refused to be paraded like livestock at the balls the other girls lived for, and Addie had reluctantly agreed. But no amount of pleas could set her free from this duty.

No doubt it was the doing of the Jackal, as she called the solicitor Francis Pemberton. She'd heard Addie more than once arguing with him behind closed doors. The conversation never varied, though the last time had been the worst.

"Keep her behavior in check, find her a husband, or I will find one for her. If that doesn't stop her delusions, I assure you I won't hesitate to have her committed. You and your brother will then be out on the street, the house and the fortune reverting to the estate."

"She is coming around, sir. And if there were an heir? Would the estate—"

"As we know, there are no heirs. I tire of this battle and these visits. Fix it, or I will."

When the door slammed, Lillian had gone into the study to find Addie sobbing gently. She'd bent next to her and held her hand. "I

32

will do better, I promise. You shall see. The Jackal will not be victorious."

"Oh, Lil, I worry for you."

Lillian shook off the memory of those difficult exchanges and tried hard to attend to the man droning on before her. Jonathan Aloysius Hoyt.

His finely cut features reminded Lillian of one of many dull portraits that graced the other homes in her fine neighborhood. Indeed, he would no doubt one day look down from a two-dimensional oil realm at his descendants carrying on their mundane existences in some well-equipped mansion. She would have nothing to do with the creation of that brood, though. She owned a mansion and wanted for nothing, except perhaps a chance to visit England again.

No, Lillian, for the first time. You have not been to London. And she wanted the Jackal to go away forever.

This man bored her to tears. When he blinked, she stole a glance at the mantel clock, wondering how time could have grown so sluggish. I *must* get back to my investigation of the Leaping Man, she thought.

Could someone actually die of boredom? The man who flew with ease from a second-story balcony would not bore her, of that she was certain. He might slit her throat instead. Of course, he would end up imprisoned someday soon, as the result of her investigation. Still, she thought Hoyt should be imprisoned for his polite drone and total disregard for the interests of his would-be object of affection. No, Hoyt could not jump from a fire landing with grace and then have the audacity to chuckle at a witness.

Lillian paused. She reminded herself that while the Leaping Man was no doubt quite clever, he was also murderer, a most loathsome creature…but clever enough to break into the mayor's mansion without creating a stir, and quite handsome. Fingers of ice ran up her back as she pictured him. What if he had chosen *her* balcony instead of her neighbor's? He must be stopped, quickly.

Without looking up from her needlework, Addie cleared her throat to signal a call to manners. Lillian's heart was to be won, she was being reminded, and her pockets were to be loosened.

Hoyt leaned in slightly—a practiced move meant to make him seem earnest. It turned Lillian's stomach.

"I said, Miss Holmes, the blossoms are most lovely this year. Would you care to take a stroll with me in the Park? Saturday promises to be an exceptionally fine day."

She caught his fleeting glance at her bodice before he sat upright and waited for her response. Damnation, she should not have let her maid pick this dress for her! It always brought excessive attention from men.

"Mr. Hoyt, I do find that blossoms are rather the same from year to year, don't you? They are pink, white, or red, open or closed to a greater or lesser degree, and give off generally the same fragrance. I have no need to see them again this year for the sake of ensuring this remains so."

Hoyt arched an eyebrow in surprise. "I see. You would perhaps rather take in the fine exhibit of Austrian paintings that is quite popular with the ladies of Baltimore just now?"

"How happy I am for the ladies of Baltimore."

"The festival at the Park tonight? I understand it will be quite a spectacle."

Lillian watched the mantel clock openly now. Her anger built. She thought of Jonathan Aloysius Hoyt's fine words, and what it would be like to have a truthful earnest suitor ask her to attend such lovely events. One who had no knowledge of her fortune, one who actually sought love and affection. One who had no knowledge of her circumstances. "Mr. Hoyt, your manners will surely secure you a fine wife one day. I suggest, however, that in the future you attend to the particulars of your dress before you call make any such attempt."

Jonathan Aloysius Hoyt blinked and sat back. "Pardon?"

"You came directly here from a house of ill repute."

"Lil! What would make you say such a thing?" Addie dropped her stitching, the color draining from her face.

"An only child with no mother…is that correct, Mr. Hoyt?"

"Well, yes, but your accusation—"

"You arrived at my door sporting several long flaxen hairs on your waistcoat, the grey clay of Fell's Point upon your soles, and the smell of rather cheap eau de toilette on your person. You are used to having your needs met by women and are exasperated at my disinterest. Sir, you are so ordinary, I will not waste a page in my journal on our meeting. Another cup of tea before you go?"

He stared at her incredulous, a flush creeping from his starched collar to his sideburns. Lillian rose and straightened her dress with as much composure as she could feign, and Hoyt stood and motioned for Thomas to bring his hat. He fled immediately thereafter.

A twinge of guilt stabbed through Lillian at her relief to be rid of him. It wasn't Mr. Hoyt's fault. It was no one's fault. She would be a spinster, and not because of this man's flaws but her nature. No man would allow his wife to pursue criminals, to favor scientific pursuits over artistic ones, to resist bowing simply because of her gender. And a husband would not want his wife to soothe her nerves with medicine, even if she were determined to give it up. Soon.

She turned to Mrs. Adencourt. "So, that is the last for the month? I have fulfilled my obligation, Addie?"

Addie covered her mouth to stifle her laughter. "I am ashamed of you, Lillian. That poor man."

"You are not ashamed. You are amused. So I think you disliked him as well." Lillian bowed and brushed her hands together in imitation of Thomas.

"Ah, my girl, what man has a chance with you?"

"The murderer has captured my full interest," Lillian announced. "Have you heard of any more crimes in the area?"

"I know it's not fear that makes you ask, and I thought we agreed you wouldn't pursue this. I don't understand your fascination with the sordid side of life, my dear. It is unnatural." Addie paused. "Your obsession with those novels is to blame, of course."

"I cannot understand your lack of interest," Lillian snapped, but she regretted it when the governess wrinkled her brow. "But then, you are the closest thing to a mother I will see on this Earth, and no daughter would want a mother to be in distress. Leave the criminals to me."

"Lillian, sit for a moment longer." The governess put down her needlepoint and faced her square on.

Lillian's heart raced, for as sure as summer would soon end Addie intended to dig deeply. *Please do not tell me more. Let's pretend for another year that we are a normal family, that I am a normal lady.* "You have my full attention, Addie."

Her governess leaned forward and put her hand on Lillian's. So rare, this contact, this longing that burned at her throat and threatened to spill over her eyelids. It would not do, not at all.

"Dear, I agree that the young men of society seem to be lacking a certain…"

"Intelligence?"

Addie didn't smile, and Lillian suppressed a shudder and turned to gaze out the window.

"Lillian, while you are too old to require instruction from a governess, I hope you still value my counsel. Is there nothing in you that desires…companionship? Do you not feel that there is a man in the world suited for you?"

"You are asking me to compromise so that the Jackal stops his pursuit."

Addie frowned and clutched her hand. "This is not about…the Jackal. I love you. I want your happiness. You don't have to be alone, Lillian. Have you never pictured yourself in the arms of some handsome fellow? Perhaps it is loneliness that causes some of your troubles."

"Is this a proper topic of discussion?" Lillian used the question as a deflection. But her mother would have asked the same, she realized, and she wondered if she would have answered differently to the woman who brought her into the world.

"Your fantasy uncle would not allow you to slip off topic so easily, would he?"

Lillian pulled her hand from Addie's and held it over her mouth to hide the quiver of her lips. Her governess's question deserved a response.

"Yes, I have thought about it from time to time," she admitted. When she was alone in bed, imagining a handsome lover hovering an inch away, pressing his lips to hers, running his strong hand down her hip. When she watched couples in the Park stealing kisses when they thought no one saw. When she read novels of love and longing… What would it be like to have a man love you and long for you?

"I know you might be afraid of men, Lil. Is it that? They are not all evil. There are good men in the world, noble men, like Thomas."

"Please, Addie. Do not fret so." Lillian forced a smile and stood to straighten her skirts. "It's simply that the right man does not knock at my door. I am sure that it will work out in due course."

Where was he, the man who did not want her money and her home, who did not require a mouse of a wife? The man who would care for a woman with a grown man's sensibilities? The man who would defend her honor rather than steal it from her?

No, do not think about it. Think instead about the Leaping Man.

"I must rush, Addie. I will continue this conversation whenever you like."

Addie sniffed out a laugh at the lie. "You have no more appointments, do you?"

"I am to meet Bess, for she would have me adjust some flaw of my appearance. I imagine it will necessitate the purchase of a new hat, as she is obsessed with hats. Then she desires to take in the Grand Festival in the Park." Lillian sighed. "I hope there will be no milliners about. Or Mr. Jonathan Aloysius Hoyt."

Addie let the last pass without comment. "You are kind, to appease your friend. I like Miss Wheeler. She has good taste in hats, and you could do with a new one. And I know you intend to buy something for her as well. You cannot hide your generosity so easily." She paused then shook her finger. "Don't go without Aileen!"

"Aileen is but twenty. She can do nothing to protect me, even though I do not need protection, and I find it unnecessary to have a maid trail along. I can open my own parasol and buy my own lemonade." *And I can use a revolver.*

"A hard life ages one. She's older and wiser than her years, and you know it."

Lillian sighed. Her maid Aileen O'Shaunessy could not emerge from their home without her ragamuffin little brothers and their friend materializing from thin air. The Musketeers, as the three boys insisted on being called, would hover around Lillian like bees on a sweet pie. Their presence brought snickers from the neighbors, but Lillian cared not. She had never found the heart to turn them away. They were good boys, despite their appearance. Still, they and their dog would not be welcome in Light Street's expensive shops.

Well, she decided, perhaps she and Bess would settle for a turn in the Park after all.

CHAPTER FOUR

A chance meeting of great importance.

"I say!" Bess called to the youngest of the Musketeers, Paddy Moran. "Control your hound! He is drooling on my only parasol."

Lillian laughed at the scene playing out in the bright midday sun. Tiny Paddy, only eight years old, struggled with Abraham, pulling at the dog's collar, but the beast was nearly as big as him. Lillian's maid, Aileen, abandoned her duties and leaned against a tree, deep in flirtation with Constable Johnnie Moran, Paddy's much older brother. As Paddy tried to gain control of Mr. Lincoln, Aileen's own younger brothers, Darby, age 11, and Billy, 13, ran along the bank of the pond, attempting to push one another into the murky waters.

The commotion of the boys was welcome to Lillian, as were the sights of the Park as it readied for the evening's festival, which was truly only an advance taste of the traveling circus arriving in Baltimore within the week. Vendors passed by selling refreshments and newspapers, an Italian organ grinder with a chirping monkey on his shoulder played joyful tunes for a penny, and romantic couples strolled slowly to stretch out their time together in the late afternoon sunshine. Lillian practiced her observational skills with each passerby, looking for minutia that others would miss.

Ah, there! The woman in purple and black stripes fidgets with her bag, looking for something while her husband surveys a toy sailboat. She deftly puts something tiny—a medicinal—into her mouth. She smiles broadly when he turns around to speak to her. A morphine addict! I, however, am not addicted to morphine, and will stop all medicinals within the month.

When the breeze blew from the west, Lillian could hear the faint strains of carousel music. The Musketeers would no doubt beg for a ride before the day was over. Everything was perfect. Except that her dearest friend was angry at her.

Bess shook her foot in annoyance, a sure sign of looming trouble. "Did I mention the hat sale was for today only?" When Bess fretted, her naturally rosy cheeks flamed, her deep blue eyes grew fierce, and her diminutive yet rounded figure seemed larger than life. The feathers of her elaborate bonnet seemed ready for flight. She would not be ignored.

"I'm sorry, Bess. I will make it up to you."

Lillian realized herself a dreadful friend. Bess asked so little, and being of a family just back from the brink of financial ruin, a sale was an important thing to her. Fashion and eligible men figured high on Bess's agenda, even if they were two topics Lillian knew nothing about.

"You will make it up to me? Of course you will. You always say that."

"I think you look quite pretty in that hat."

Bess sighed. "We both know that I am not pretty, but I appreciate the sentiment."

"Nonsense."

"You don't understand, Lil. You are so beautiful. How could you know what it is to be a cripple, to not have fine features and a perfect figure? Once again, I didn't receive an invitation to the Swanson Ball. They would not have an ugly girl dragging her club foot around their dance floor."

"Nor would they have me, thank God. I suppose they think me a lunatic. So we'll spend that night doing something marvelous, how would that be? We could take in the symphony!"

Bess's eyes grew glassy and Lillian dreaded the coming tears. She had run out of platitudes since the day they'd become friends. She'd pulled the slow and clumsy Bess away from an oncoming trolley. The poor thing had tripped, cut her head and torn her dress. Lillian had hailed a hansom cab and helped patch and clean the stranger up in her nearby home. The bond was since unbroken.

The two loneliest women in Baltimore, Bess liked to say: one too ugly and poor for a man of society, one too intelligent. But in truth, Lillian admired Bess's quick wit and sharp mind, and treasured her loyalty. If only she could persuade Bess to begin learning about science and human nature, she would have the perfect ally for her investigations.

"Where are you, Lillian? You're already dreaming about some phantom adventure, aren't you?"

"I am sorry. How can I make it up to you? Name the day and time."

"Aha! I will!" Bess's scowl turned to a mischievous grin and she turned to face her, one gloved hand on Lillian's sleeve. "I know you will not approve, but you gave your word." Her cheeks dimpled with her smile, and her curls bobbed with her excitement. She pulled a folded flier from her bag and handed it over.

Lillian unfolded the flier littered with mysterious symbols and sketches of the constellations. "Madam Pelosi? Oh, no!"

"Do read on."

"Spiritualist extraordinaire. Urgent messages from the dead… Oh, Bess, no, no. Why do you invest your energies this way?"

Bess pulled Lillian's book from her hands and tapped the frontispiece in reply. "*A Study of the Poisons of Indochine*. I wish you would read something less…deadly. Haven't you memorized that book yet? How can you invest *your* energies this way? Why must you know about poisons, the weapons of India, the nature of soils? I know you are brilliant, but you must also *live*."

Lillian didn't know what that meant anymore. "It *is* my life, Bess. I don't know another way to live."

Her friend sighed and squeezed her arm. "I do not mean to be cruel. You teach me to reach for more than a pretty hat and a slick-tongued suitor. Still, I imagine I will spend my days as a hatless old maid, chiding you and accepting your charity."

"I will not let that happen," Lillian said. She closed her book and withdrew a smaller notebook from her bag. "I will find you a suitable companion. I will put it on my list."

"Your list?"

"My list of life goals. You must start one. How do you prioritize your time? I will put finding you a husband above learning German."

"You are incredibly thoughtful." Bess wiggled her foot vigorously.

A loud commotion broke their argument as Abraham barked and one of the boys splashed in the pond, cursing at his brother. Johnnie and Aileen rushed to sort out the chaos and pull him from the water. Lillian just shook her head in amusement.

"Constable Moran seems to spend all of his time rescuing the same three young men from themselves," Bess observed.

Lillian nodded. "He's a good man for Aileen. They are in the same predicament, are they not? Trying to raise younger siblings on their own. I approve of the match and have told Aileen as much."

"Oh, no! Abraham now drips with mud. My dress is doomed."

Lillian barely heard her friend, as her attention was drawn from the ragamuffins to a couple passing from beneath the ornamental arch. The pair emerged and stopped up the path to enjoy the comedic scene at the pond. Lillian was drawn to the man, as something in his figure struck a familiar chord. About her age, he radiated a calm ease rather than practiced poise.

Bess held her hand up to her mouth and whispered behind it, "Do you know him? I must meet him. Who's the girl? Hopefully a younger sister. What shall I do to meet him?"

Lillian glanced over. "Why must you meet him? You are confusing me, Bess."

"Are you blind? Don't you think he's the most handsome fellow ever?"

"*Ever?* Surely you do not mean that literally." Though, he might be the most handsome man Lillian had seen that day or the day before. "No, they are surely not brother and sister, as their coloring could not be more unlike. Betrothed. In love. But something is off here... Ah, she is new to wealth. She does not wear the hat properly, has not been trained to walk properly. Her boots are scuffed, even though the dress is new."

He *is* comely, Lillian admitted to herself, watching further. Coal-black hair and brows, bright blue eyes and fine jaw line. He cut quite the figure as he leapt to the aid of Paddy, who struggled once again to control Abraham, and an unfamiliar flutter in her stomach made her blush. Lillian pushed down an urge to straighten her hat and ensure her dress was unwrinkled. No man was worth that vanity.

He jumped again to retrieve the hound, and Lillian's blood ran cold. Surely there was more than one young man in Baltimore who moved in such a graceful, athletic manner. He was the same height and build as the Leaping Man...

No, this man was an inch or two shorter.

Don't be ridiculous, Lillian. This is not your man.

The stranger held the beast firmly as he chatted with the constable, whom he seemed to know. Then Lillian's bench was suddenly surrounded by her maid Aileen, Constable Moran, the wet and chagrined Musketeers, and their muddy hound. Bess jumped to her feet and scurried to the back of the bench in an attempt to stay clean. Lillian rose to greet the strangers who approached just a few steps behind.

What should I say, what should I ask? He might recognize me if he is the murderer. And if so, would he dare approach me in broad daylight?

The stranger regarded Lillian for a fleeting moment with a subtle bow of the head before speaking again to the constable, and Lillian understood for the first time what a twinkle of the eye meant. This man's eyes had come alive when he glanced at her, if he quickly hooded them in mystery, his long dark lashes brushing his very pale cheeks. He was quite unusual, and his aura toyed with a distant memory of early childhood, one Lillian couldn't bring into focus. Could he be a long-lost relative? She would have to ask Addie, if indeed her governess would speak on the subject.

Constable Johnnie Moran rubbed at his chin in confusion, as if he were desperately trying to remember a protocol he probably never learned. Lillian liked Johnnie, and she decided it was time to rescue him.

"Allow me to introduce Miss Elisabeth Wheeler, my dear friend." She indicated Bess, who had suddenly overcome her fear of mud to scurry forward to stand before the strangers. The man bowed deeply and touched her hand when she offered it. "I am Lillian Holmes. Aileen O'Shaunessy, in my employ. Her brothers, Darby and Billy. You seem to know Officer Moran and his young brother Paddy. You have certainly met Mr. Abraham Lincoln."

Johnnie snapped out of his stupor. "So sorry, Miss Holmes. May I introduce Mr. Phillip Orleans and Miss Mary Catherine Twamley."

Lillian stared into Mr. Orleans's eyes, daring him to exhibit a flash of recognition. The man held her stare for a moment, until Bess pulled at her sleeve.

"Lillian, please, what has gotten into you? We are happy to make your acquaintance. Are you from Baltimore, Miss Twamley?"

"No, Miss Wheeler, but it has been my home these many years." The woman smiled broadly, matching the expression in her lovely lilting voice and eyes.

"Twamley, Twamley..." Lillian noticed Kitty's smile widen. "Ah, the artist Kitty Twamley?"

Bess squealed. "Truly? You were the talk of the Artists' Tent at the Exhibition this year!"

Kitty beamed. "You are too kind. I am still learning."

Lillian blew out the breath she was holding. This couple was not murderous in the least. The young lady, although not born to society, was pleasant. Her companion seemed a bit more aloof but not her Leaping Man. Too short, too thin, and somehow lacking the devilish quality she'd seen that night.

Kitty whispered something into the man's ear, and he took a moment before nodding and turning to address Lillian.

"Ladies, an acquaintance of Kitty's graces us with a visit for one week only and will be entertaining us on Saturday evening. I know we have just met, but Kitty is quite anxious to complete the party, and we do seem to be neighbors."

Lillian's heart dropped. A social engagement. One that required small talk with shallow, boring strangers. But Bess, oh, Bess would want to go.

"She sings? She dances? Pray tell, what kind of performance?"

"Madam Annaluisa Pelosi is a popular medium we befriended while on a recent trip to New Orleans. While I have little interest in such things—"

He was drowned out by Bess's squeals. "Oh! We'll come. Lillian, you promised me. What an amazing coincidence."

Kitty clapped her hands happily. "Do come, Miss. I rarely have visitors, so preoccupied with my painting... I..."

Ah, she lacks female companions. Lillian pushed down a sigh. How could she be so dour and selfish with two other young ladies giggling with excitement?

"Splendid, then!" Phillip said. "I will send a carriage for you. Johnnie, would you like to come and bring Aileen?"

"Would you like to attend?" Lillian asked the maid, but she also warned Aileen off with a quick movement of her eyes. While she did not feel the need to keep the girl in her place, such an outing would regretfully elicit another tiresome conversation with Addie about propriety.

"Oh, no, Miss, I have other duties." Aileen curtsied quickly, and Lillian knew she understood.

"Then you needn't bother with a carriage," she said to Phillip, "as Bess and I enjoy walking."

The man handed her a card with his address on it, and then, with a quick tip of his hat, he ushered Kitty down the path and away.

When the couple was out of earshot and Johnnie returned to his beat, Lillian gathered the Musketeers. The filthy crew got in line, Mr. Lincoln at the end, wagging his muddy tail. Lillian smiled inwardly, knowing how excited the boys were. Whenever she lined them up, it meant the promise of sweets or pennies.

"Listen carefully, boys."

"Musketeers," Paddy corrected and then sucked at his thumb.

"That's quite right, Patrick Moran! One penny to each of you who brings to me a stunning piece of information about Mr. Phillip Orleans before Saturday. What are the rules?"

Aileen's brother Billy jumped up and down.

"Yes, Billy, before you burst."

"Not one bit of hearsay. No gossip from young ladies. No gossip from old ladies, unless they are servants in his employ." He paused and scratched his head as if the effort were almost too much.

"And the greatest rule of all?"

"Be safe! We are not to be seen, to leave the neighborhood, or to steal."

"Very good. You will stay together, obey Aileen and Constable Moran, and stay out of trouble."

Paddy moved forward and pulled at her skirt. "Can we come to the dinner with you? Abraham will stay outside."

"I am sorry, but you may not come. However, I will ask Addie to have a fine cake made for you on Saturday. And you all may have dinner at my home with Aileen that evening. Perhaps Aileen will ask Constable Moran to join her. Please be sure to wash before Saturday, boys. You smell of pond."

Abraham chose that moment to rid himself of the mud he'd acquired with a vigorous shake, transferring most of it to Bess's yellow dress.

"I say, Lil! Now you owe me a new dress as well as a husband. Please put *that* on your life list."

"I will replace the dress," Lillian said. "Of course I will."

Bess seemed mollified. "Kitty is sweet, isn't she? If she weren't, I would poison her drink on Saturday to free Mr. Orleans to be my husband. Do you think I could manage it? You know all about undetectable poisons from your Sherlock Holmes books, do you not? Of course, he would have to be daft or blind to want me."

Lillian frowned and adjusted one of her friend's blond ringlets. "I do not think him suitable for you or for Kitty. You do not want that man."

"Why do I not? I think I would very much like that man. He is handsome, certainly wealthy, and he seems kind and intelligent."

"Bess, a lion in the jungle is rather handsome as well, except to the gazelle he takes down with his sharp claws and teeth. Phillip Orleans looks very much like someone I saw recently..." She stopped herself. Not even Bess would believe her. Or, out of concern Bess would speak to Addie, and then Dr. Schneider *would* lower the boom. Thinking swiftly, Lillian changed tack and said, "Perhaps we will seek the counsel of Madam Pelosi in matters of your future husband. Now, let's attend to that dress."

***

The evening was as hot and cloudless as the day. Bess pulled Lillian along from this tent to that vendor, every which way, so excited to be out and about in a crowd. She squealed in front of a colorfully striped tent and squeezed Lillian's arm. "Oh! We found her!"

"I see why you are here, Elisabeth." Lillian pointed to the sign announcing Madam Pelosi's talents and sighed. Wasn't it enough that they would be entertained by this charlatan on Saturday night? There was a short line of people waiting to experience the magic for themselves. "Your romantic life is not in the hands of the spirit world. I entreat you to walk with me and save your coin."

Bess frowned and stomped her good foot. "Your promises are very short-lived, Lil. You owe me several gay evenings, a dress and a hat, and if memory serves—"

"And it always does."

"—a trip to the seaside as a reward for dressing as a charwoman and following that poor, *innocent* Chinaman about last summer."

"Well, I was mistaken about him. I was certain that was a disguise. In any case, I suggest a compromise. Walk with me a bit, and we will return shortly to end our adventure at this tent. I would like a cool drink first."

"You know I do not like to walk far."

"Just a bit. Come now, be brave and proud!"

Lillian marveled at the transformation of her neighborhood park—indeed, it belonged to all of Baltimore, though she'd come to think of it as her personal garden, as it nearly fronted her home. Tonight strains of calliope music fought with a marching band playing the latest Sousa tune in the distance, and were punctuated by the squeals of children's laughter.

Bess clapped as a juggler threw flaming torches high into the air. A man dressed in Chinese silks and a grotesque mask walked past them on stilts in the unsettling gait of a giant insect. "Perhaps *he* is your criminal. Would you have me follow him as well?" she chided.

Their attention was drawn to a hundred marvels, and Lillian, much to her own surprise, found that she was enjoying the night immensely. She only thought of the Leaping Man every half hour or so.

Bess adjusted Lillian's feathered hat and linked her arm through hers. "Isn't this better than reading a pamphlet on soils or mollusks or the history of the Hindus? Why must you always wear deep blue? You look as if you're in mourning. How lovely you'd look in white. I know, quite impractical. You're so beautiful, Lillian. Why must you ignore your appearance? Now your hat has gone quite floppy again."

"I've gone quite floppy in this heat. At least I didn't wear a corset. You must be ready to faint. Although I must say you look rather pretty in all that pink, like a small party cake from Eisner's bakery."

"No corset?" Bess's blonde curls bobbed as she shook her head in frustration. "Didn't Aileen dress you tonight? What am I to do with you?"

Bess regaled Lillian with details of the coming circus, but Lillian only took in half of what she said. Several feet away, a young boy of no more than eight, dressed in near rags that hung limply on his thin torso, pretended to watch a shell game at a nearby table. He was giving quick glances at a gentleman whose senses were entirely focused on the chap running the game.

I see you, little man.

In a practiced nonchalant move, the urchin backed into the gentleman, apologized, and moved deftly behind a nearby tree. Lillian dashed after him and clamped onto his arm before he could flee. She squatted down and stared into his widened eyes.

"Yes, miss?" He trembled, eyes darting about to plan his escape.

Lillian held her palm out. The boy bit at his lip and dropped the watch and fob into her hand.

"I am going to count. If you are not far from this park by the time I reach twenty, you shall certainly be sorry. Do you understand?" She kept a tight grip on the boy's arm.

"Lillian, surely you must report him," Bess whispered, appearing from around the side of the tree.

"Surely you know he is too young for prison, where he will no doubt live someday," Lillian whispered back. Then, to the quivering boy she said, "One," and he was off like a rabbit.

Lillian handed the watch and fob to Bess with the instruction to return them to the owner before she spun to address the busy table with the shell game. She pushed her way directly to the front and picked up the thimblerigger's three thimbles, creating a scene among his unsuspecting patrons.

The thimblerigger's face flushed scarlet in anger. "What are you thinking there? Give me those back. I have a business to run."

"Your business is a fraud. Your son is a shill and a pickpocket. I would encourage your customers to move along and enjoy the music."

Bess linked them arm in arm to pull Lillian away from the burly man. "That's enough, Lil. We must hurry, or we'll not have time for our psychic readings." As they made their escape she added, "How did you know it was his son?"

"How could you not know?"

"You must be more discreet. Now that carnie is angry at you, and if your neighbors are about they'll tell Addie or even the Jackal about your shenanigans."

"Stopping a theft is not shenanigans. The Jackal, as a lawyer, albeit a terrible one in my estimation, could not even argue that point."

They bought lemons with peppermint stick straws and strolled back to the medium's tent. A patron emerged, and with no one else in line Bess steeled herself for her long-desired reading.

"I shall wait here," Lillian ventured.

"No, please! What if she imparts terrible news? I would want you nearby."

Bess pulled at Lillian's arm and drew back the tent flap. The cloying smell of candles and incense assaulted them as the contents of the darkened tent came into focus, and Bess cried out at the otherworldly images that danced on a screen set up on one side of the tent.

"Bess, it's a phantasmagoria, a projection, designed to instill fear and wonder. Ignore the images." At the same time Lillian wondered how Mr. Conan Doyle could be so taken with this type of amusement. Surely he did not believe in anything but the here and now, as did Uncle Sherlock.

She started at the astounding vision of Madam Pelosi and her ridiculous costume: a multicolored suit of varying fabrics, a tall black hat with a meshed veil pulled across her cheeks, enough kohl on her eyes for a wagon of gypsies. The woman was more frightful even than the phantasmagoria.

Lillian took Bess's hand. "I think we have made a mistake."

The medium smiled, bringing deep dimples to life. "What sort of mistake, Miss Holmes?" Then she patted the table in a merry fashion with her black lace gloves and gestured for them to sit.

Bess tightened her grip on Lillian's hand and whispered, "She knows your name, Lil!"

"I would think that her friend Kitty Twamley is skilled at description. Is that not so, Madam Pelosi?"

"Do call me Anna. My friends do, and my hope is that we shall become friends. Kitty described you both perfectly, which is her habit as she is an artist."

Lillian sighed and examined the counterfeit antiquities for sale on a display table and shelves above it.

"Of course, Mr. Orleans said that you were both beautiful women of society."

"How generous," Lillian mumbled.

"Now, Miss Wheeler, since Miss Holmes is not a believer, I assume you are the one with questions for the spirit world?"

Bess stepped forward and nodded eagerly.

As her friend discussed with Anna what manner of communication would be best for the divination of her future, Lillian continued to survey the medium's possessions: jars of crushed stones and colorful viscous liquids that vied for shelf space with talismans from the corners of the world, miniature obelisks and pyramids, and even a few fragments that appeared to be mummified human fingers and toes.

"We are ready, Miss Holmes," Anna announced. "Won't you join us?"

Lillian took a seat and watched carefully for the medium's tricks. Madam Pelosi closed her eyes and hummed lowly, swaying to and fro. Bess seemed mesmerized, but Lillian recognized the tune as a southern Negro cakewalk rather than a mysterious chant of the Orient.

As if she truly read minds, Anna opened her eyes suddenly and stared at Lillian. "I am simply clearing my head. The tune is not important." She pulled out a leather bound notebook, flattened it open to a fresh page, and dipped her pen in a bronze inkwell. "Miss Wheeler, ask three questions and I will lift the veil to allow the spirits to answer."

Lillian snickered. "Will the spirits write in English or Italian, Miss Pelosi?"

Bess was undeterred. She leaned in to whisper her questions in Anna's ear.

Immediately, the mystic wrote in a flourishing script, not stopping for a full minute. "There!" she said when through. "Simple enough. You are favored, Miss Wheeler. The spirits are happy to report that, aside from your gait, you are sound of health, will live a happy life, and bear several healthy children. You will find a good match within the year."

Bess let out a gasp and quickly covered her mouth to hide how pleased she was.

Lillian held back a cluck of disdain and rose to leave. Any simpleton would know the right answers to give an unmarried young woman. "Since I owe you several debts, Elisabeth, allow me to pay for your reading."

"There is no charge, Miss Holmes, as we have a mutual friend. Now it is your turn."

"No, thank you."

"Are you quite sure? The spirit world dictated for you as well. I believe we have contacted one of your dearly departed relatives. Your mother, perhaps?"

Anna turned the notebook around and stared into Lillian's eyes until gooseflesh rose on her flesh and her legs turned to soft taffy. The light reflecting on her face made her look deathly pale beneath her heavy makeup, and her breath seemed to take on shape, as if they sat out in freezing winter.

Bess linked her arm through Lillian's. "Miss Pelosi, that is a delicate matter. Lillian is more sensitive on this subject than she might appear."

"I assure you, it is not meant in jest."

Lillian eyed the scrawl and felt frozen, afraid to look, unable to turn away. No, the mother she did not remember would not speak to this charlatan. But she struggled to hold back a tear as she leaned in and squinted to take in the words.

As she finished reading the first phrase, *Beware, my love,* the script faded quickly until she saw only a blank page.

Lillian sat up straight and gathered herself. "Disappearing ink from beyond the grave, Miss Pelosi?"

The woman frowned and examined her bronze inkpot. "Heartfelt apologies, Miss Holmes. I am sure I filled the pot with India ink. How unfortunate." She pinched the bridge of her turned-up nose and blew out a deep breath. "I cannot remember what I wrote. That is the nature of the communication. It is a trance, you see."

"How inconvenient," Lillian retorted.

"Oh, now, don't be angry. We will meet again at the Orleans home, where I shall make it right." She offered her gloved hand, which Lillian shook.

Bess and Lillian left the tent. As arm in arm they wound their way up to Eutaw Street, Lillian kept silent, mulling over the strange encounter with Madam Annaluisa Pelosi. At least, she admitted, her friend was happy knowing her future was secure.

CHAPTER FIVE

He stoops to conquer.

"No, I won't do it." George tapped his brother in the back with his walking stick to punctuate each word.

"You said you'd enjoy hunting with me again. Blazes, George, I'm usually snug in my bed by this hour."

"It's not my fault you prefer daylight and I dislike it."

Phillip sneered. "You created me. Now hold a cloth over your nose. You asked for one week to prove your sincerity. I intend to fully test your character change."

George stared at the gruesome sight before them. A young man lay on the dock, having taken a bullet to his torso. He wore the clothes of a sailor, with the grime and stench of the harbor covering his clothes, and he was near death, given the amount of blood seeping out of him. Next to him, his small roll of belongings had been rifled through, and no doubt any valuables whisked into the night by his attacker.

"Perhaps he's dead."

"He's not dead and you know it. He's suffering."

"Then we should call for a physician."

"Stop it! He has a few minutes. And we could be after his attacker, you know. Although it's likely too late for that."

"After his attacker? It's not enough that you feast on the damned, you also try to right society's wrongs? Will you become a barrister next? Perhaps open a home for sailors and orphans?"

"I'm immune to your insults, as you well know."

"God, this is a hard bargain." George steeled himself for the stench and knelt by the victim. "My appetite is nearly spoiled." But he lied. He'd not fed for the two days he'd been back in the house with Phillip.

He knelt down and lifted the dying lad into his arms. Their gazes held for a moment before George pushed the sailor's face to the side and slid his teeth into that barely pulsing neck. But the rush of energy through his veins was tainted as he drank, tainted with the act of helping usher this man out of pain. His eyes had said it all. *"Help me."*

George did. When he wiped his mouth and stood, he turned away from Phillip's annoying watchfulness.

"See, you survived."

George shrugged off Phillip's hand and strode along the dock.

"Oh, come on, Georgy. I've seen you do far lower things."

Aye, they'd all *been lower.* Had he felt sympathy before this night? What a hellish bargain this would be, far worse than he anticipated. "I'm going home. Enough for one night. I need a bath."

"That's fine. Now, to impress Kitty a bit more, you'll have to socialize with us. It will take some masterful acting on your part to be less of a bore—"

"A bore!"

Phillip smiled, and George couldn't help but smirk back. It *was* good to be with him again, even under these intolerable circumstances.

"Yes, we're entertaining on Saturday. You remember Madam Pelosi from New Orleans, don't you? She'll be there, and a few new friends of Kitty's."

"Annaluisa is not so bad. I might be able to stomach it. Are Kitty's 'new friends' attractive in any way? This diet of rotting male flesh doesn't satisfy any of my appetites."

"You will stomach it, and you'll be kind to our guests. And do make sure you fill up before they arrive."

George groaned and brushed at his sleeves. "I offer no guarantees. I thirst, verily I thirst."

"Yes, well, verily satisfy that thirst in Fell's Point. And remember our agreement. I don't have time to watch you every second."

"I will find the most heinous criminal in Baltimore."

"Yes, well, that would be *you,* now, wouldn't it? Just be bathed and dressed before the party."

CHAPTER SIX

The Talking Cure.

Lillian closed her eyes and listened to the tapping noise from the secretary's type-writing machine in the next room. Fretting that the work might contain the doctor's notes about her, she wondered if she could determine what was being typed by the distinct sound of the keys.

No, impossible. It was not Morse code, which she had studied in the summer should she ever need to send secret messages to an assistant. She snickered, remembering how infuriated Bess became when she insisted she too learn the system. "When you learn to dance, I will learn your secret code." Bess hated Lillian's sleuthing, hated everything about it. No, that wasn't quite true. Bess worried that her sleuthing would cause more trouble for her. Of course, it seemed she might be right.

Dr. Schneider tapped on the door and entered the subtly lit sitting room, and Lillian forced the topic of sleuthing from her mind. It would not do at all to mention it to this gentle but astute man.

"And here we are, my dear." He pulled a pencil from his jacket pocket, squinted over his glasses at his notes, and seemed far away.

"*Guten Tag*, Herr Doctor Schneider," Lillian offered her hand.

"Yes, yes indeed." Instead of shaking her hand, he took her pulse. "How are your nerves, Miss Holmes? Did you race here today?"

Oh, blazes! Now the talking cure will commence. If he tries to hypnotize you, you will resist, you will play the role but stay alert.

"Yes, yes, I did race. So many people about at this time of day. I had to dodge between carriages… Oh, such a rush!"

He sat across from her and peered over his glasses intently. *Damnation.* But the man didn't read minds, although he likely tried.

"Tell me what transpired since we last met. Are you sleeping well?"

"Except for those few frightfully hot nights, yes, I am."

"And what else? How have you spent your time?"

"On feminine pursuits of the ordinary kind: shopping with my friend Elisabeth, taking in the festival, that sort of thing."

The doctor sat back in the chair and lit his pipe. "Indeed, I am sure you have done those things. And I would be pleased if that were the full extent of it. But Mrs. Adencourt, as you know, is somewhat concerned for you. Should she be? I must make a report to Mr. Pemberton on your progress, you know."

Lillian sighed. Of course. As she'd expected. Addie meant well, would probably die for her. A shiver shimmied up her spine. Why had she thought of Addie dying? *I must find the Leaping Man. Now I worry for my loved ones.*

"What are you thinking about now, Miss Holmes?"

"That Addie should not fear, at least where my well-being is concerned."

"What should she fear? God knows the criminals have been quite busy. Has this affected you at all?"

"Not at all."

"And you've been writing in your journal as we discussed? Has it helped calm your nerves?"

"I have written daily."

"Wunderbar! Tell me one topic you committed to your journal."

Mr. Nosey Parker. "Nothing comes to mind of any import."

"I see. Lillian, dear, we have known one another for several years. I have bandaged cuts from daggers, a bullet wound to the foot…"

"I was just learning to shoot!"

"As I was saying, knife wounds, a bullet wound, a severe episode of wasting when you forgot to eat for many days, so absorbed in your studies were you. You are among my most intelligent, adventurous patients. But I cannot help you if you don't let me."

Ah, so he will not even mention the worst of it. As if it never happened, as if my baby never existed. But she did, certainly she did. The awful possibility that she'd imagined her too made Lillian sit up straight, her nerves on fire. No! She was certain.

"I do not need help! I am fit, healthier than most; I do not suffer in any way! I value your help, Doctor, but I assure you, I would know if I were ill."

"When was the last time you bought a medicinal of any kind?"

There, he'd finally gotten to it. The moment she knew would come. She'd steeled herself for it. "I don't remember. That is no longer an issue for me."

"This morning, Miss Holmes. You have forgotten an important part of deduction, of the observation that you love so much. You have forgotten that others may practice it as well. It is my profession. The signs are there, in your pupils, in the way you moisten your mouth, in the quick movements of your hands, in your rapid heartbeat.

"We are both too intelligent to continue this game. I know you, and you will try to stop taking the drug on your own, quickly. That will make you sick, and very weak, and—listen carefully, Lillian—if you have been indulging frequently and stop suddenly…you could die. Your heart could stop beating. Is this not the business of your physician? Do you see why I pry?"

Lillian nodded. *I started to stop the Melancholies, but they never went away.* "The Melancholies never went away." She put her hand over her mouth, shocked that she'd uttered the words. A tear slipped down her cheek and she brushed at it.

Dr. Schneider sat back and tented his hands on his large stomach, tapping his fingers together. "These melancholies, as you say. Do you know what causes them?"

"I am not sure." The tears horrified Lillian, as they would not stop no matter how she willed them to do so. *Please do not lock me away with the lunatics. I am sane.*

"We cannot cure a disease until we identify it. Surely your Mister Holmes would concur."

"True."

"Good, we have a goal. We will strive to understand these melancholies, and we will plan a course of treatment to free you from your 'medication.' It will necessitate the slow weaning off of opiates. You are to only take pills that I prescribe for you, and in the precise number and at the precise times I instruct. Are you willing to try?"

No. Leave me alone. But you will not. Addie will not. Bess will not. The Jackal will hound me until I cannot stand another day of it, and he will convince you to send me away. I must appear agreeable.

"I am willing to try."

"Wunderbar!" Dr. Schneider took both her hands and squeezed them in a fatherly way that made her tears flow more. "It will be fine, my dear. Now, how did you get that cut on your wrist?"

"I… Oh, I may as well tell you. I was poking about on a neighbor's fire escape and slipped. A nail was protruding. It is a long tale." And she wasn't going to tell him that she'd been examining the dirt left by the Leaping Man's shoes.

"Ah, an investigation. You are worse than my youngest son. Please be more careful next time. It looks inflamed. Let's get more light on it…"

Lillian smiled, for he had not reprimanded her for her investigation. What would it be like to talk freely of her studies, to live openly, to be alive, fully alive? Perhaps he could help her. But could she trust him?

"Yes," she announced. "I will be more careful."

***

"Enter," Lillian answered Aileen's peculiar four-tap knock, and the maid immediately walked to the armoire to pick out a dress for dinner. Lillian had spent the last hour writing at her desk, putting to paper all she knew of the Leaping Man. Her heart raced with the thought of seeing Mr. Orleans this evening. He *could* have a connection to the Leaping Man. The resemblance was there.

"The sapphire, Miss?" Aileen's voice bore the mildest tone of reproof, as if to add, "Won't you please buy another evening dress!"

"I take your point, Aileen. No doubt you and Miss Wheeler go on behind my back about my disregard for fashion."

"Never! I wouldn't treat you so, Lil. I mean, *Miss.* Please, tell me you don't think that about me."

Lillian took her seat before the dresser to allow the maid to fuss with her hair. She looked up and smiled. "I'm teasing."

To her shock, Aileen seemed to be holding back tears. No, there it was: a lone drop trickled down her freckled cheek. And Aileen's pale blue eyes were rimmed in red to match the fiery red curls that often escaped her white cap.

Lillian turned and took the maid's hand. "I assure you, Aileen, I was teasing! Your position is secure here. I know how badly you need this work. You are my friend, are you not?"

"I'm sorry, Miss. I don't mean trouble." She broke into sobs and covered her face.

Lillian pulled her hands away and led her to the bed, forcing her to sit. "You must not take things to heart so."

"It's not you, Miss. It's the boys," she managed between sobs. "They're being turned out. Old Breuner is closing his tannery and can't use them. It's not only the pittance he pays them; they've been sleeping there. Johnnie would take them in to live with him and Paddy, but they are not allowed to have four live in the one room." Aileen covered her mouth to stifle her sobs.

Orphans to poverty, Lillian thought. Aileen's parents had died of tuberculosis within a few months of one another, shortly after the birth of their youngest, Darby. *I too am an orphan.* Without her inheritance, she might be in the same position as Aileen. Or worse. With no skill in dressing a young lady, she would have no doubt been as good as a slave, scrubbing floors or working in the oyster cannery.

She strode to the door and called loudly for Thomas.

The butler appeared as quickly as his lame leg would carry him up the grand staircase. Eyes wide, he looked inside the room. "What's the racket, Miss? I thought you saw a murderer!"

"Clear the storage room, Thomas. Put the things in the kitchen, or anywhere you like. Put down two pallets and a stand. The room has a small window, does it not? Addie will know what to do. The remaining O'Shaunessys will be employed here, for room and board, starting this evening."

"Miss, you cannot mean those rapscallions... Beggin' your pardon, Aileen, but—"

"Let them do the work that causes your leg to hurt. It will be a boon for all involved. That is enough, Thomas."

The butler cursed softly and turned.

Lillian called him back. "By the way, have you finished that collapsing spyglass I fancy?"

"Not yet, Miss," he replied, with a tone that said he'd prefer to finish it when pigs took flight. Then he limped and mumbled all the way down the stairs. He would not mistreat the boys, but he would likely need to replenish his whiskey stock more often.

Aileen fell upon her with hugs, clutching at her shoulders and sobbing still. "You have a kind soul, Lillian Holmes. If there were any other way, I would turn away your offer."

"This is nothing, put it out of your mind. Now, hurry with my hair, for we've wasted a good amount of time with all this fretting."

"Yes, Miss."

"Aileen, one more thing. Mr. Abraham Lincoln does not enter the house. It is one thing to replace Bess's best frock, another to answer to Addie over ruined furniture. You may keep him in the yard. When the cold weather arrives…well, we shall formulate a plan then for the hound. We both know that, while I am the lady of the house, there is one above me."

"Oh, you aren't lying! I mean, yes, Miss."

"Next week, I will give you money to buy new dresses, one day dress and one evening. You know my measurements. Bess will be thrilled to help you. You may buy yourself a little something as well, and I do owe one to Bess in addition. And some new shoes for the boys, if you can convince them to wear shoes. Yes, let us make that a house rule. The boys will have shoes."

"Oh! A lovely emerald silk, cut low and… This mane of black will shine against the green."

"Why must it be cut low? Everything you have made for me is cut low!"

It seemed the maid was in a hurry to see her married as well. What a horrid way to find a husband, exposing one's bosom.

Aileen hummed as she pinned Lillian's hair, one long lock at a time. "Mr. Orleans is quite handsome, Miss. And so is his older brother I hear from Johnnie, as far as men can be trusted in such matters. Johnnie says they have a good deal of money. More than a good deal. They own a shipyard. And it's said that their home is filled with priceless…obj…*things*, especially French things."

"*Objets d'art*. How nice for the Orleans brothers. Does Johnnie also believe I should find a husband in the Orleans household?"

Aileen flushed and dropped the subject.

Ah, I hear Bess. And if I'm not mistaken, my Musketeers are trailing along. Hopefully Mr. Lincoln has not come inside."

Lillian descended to the parlor, kissed her friend and lined the boys up by height. Billy, Darby, and Paddy. They each saluted.

"Yes, my Musketeers?"

Paddy wiggled in excitement, barely able to contain himself, but as usual Billy would speak for the trio. "The baker Jacob Eisner says that he heard from a maid who lives near Orleans that a carriage driver saw—"

"Stop right there. Did you forget the definition of the word hearsay?"

Billy stared at the ceiling for rescue. Darby looked at his feet.

Lillian paced with her hands behind her back as Uncle Sherlock did when he lectured on a topic. It felt quite right to, she thought. She made a mental note to add the practice in all appropriate situations.

Paddy squirmed and squealed for more attention, finally raising his hand and jumping up and down.

Lillian nodded. "Go ahead."

"I did the best, I really did! You promised a penny, but this is worth at least two. I followed him and another man. They're brothers, that's what they call each other. I followed them all evening, and they didn't see me once, no they didn't. What do you think of that?" He put his hands on his hips and bit his lip, anxious to tell the rest.

"I'm concerned that you did so at night, but go on."

"First I asked Johnnie where fine men like them might spend their time, saying I wouldn't mind being a fine man. Johnnie called me a loon first, but then he told me that he had no idea where they might go, perhaps to a cigar parlor."

Darby punched Paddy in the arm, which starting a shoving match. Lillian cleared her throat and held up three pennies.

"So I followed them."

"Yes, we gathered that. Quickly, where did they go?" Lillian squatted to face him at eye level.

Paddy closed his eyes to concentrate. "They walked so fast, Miss. All the way down to the Light Street wharfs."

Bess clucked. "That is too far! You're not to go to the wharfs!"

Lillian hushed her, and the boy shrugged.

"And then?" Lillian prompted.

"They went into a place with music and loud men, and I didn't see them after that. I waited a long time, though."

Lillian groaned and turned to Bess. "See why I must do this myself? Details, there are no details!"

"It's not Paddy's fault that men frequent harbor dens. And do you see why the boys cannot continue to do this? Paddy is only eight! How horrid would you feel if he'd been hurt?"

Paddy shuffled his feet. "It's not worth a penny?"

"Of course you'll get your penny. Now, off with all of you. Find Aileen or Thomas and see if they need help around the house. Darby and Billy, you are to stay with your sister here from now on; Thomas is preparing a room for you. If you do not behave, you will answer to Mrs. Adencourt."

Billy and Darby hugged Lillian's skirts, which threw her off balance, mentally and physically. Then the boys ran outside, surely looking for mischief rather than work, and Lillian sat next to Bess.

"I see more of your generosity at work here. The boys do love you," her friend announced. "The Adencourts love you, too. As does Aileen. And I love you, Lil."

Lillian's stomach churned, for she knew what Bess was saying: *Don't put yourself in harm's way. You are falling back into your fantasy world.* Dr. Schneider's words, the Jackal's words, Addie's words, and now Bess.

"I love you as well."

"It's not appropriate to follow a man—" Bess suddenly sighed, knowing that propriety was the last thing Lillian cared about. "Lil…"

"Yes?"

"Have you been taking your medicine? When did you last visit with Doctor Schneider?" Her lips twitched with nervousness.

"I am fine, Bess."

"Your eyes… I am sorry, Lil, but your eyes do not look fine. In moments we are to go to the Orleans function. I do not think it is wise to do so. I will stay here with you and send a note."

"I am fine! You are dying to go and chat with Kitty and the rest. What makes you say such nonsense?" But, oh God, her friend would give up what she craved most because she feared for Lillian's sanity? Lillian vowed to meet with the doctor again. This slow weaning from her medicine would kill her. In fact, she'd inadvertently doubled her dose, having forgotten today she'd already taken it. But what would it truly hurt? Dr. Schneider had stressed that she should lessen use gradually, after all.

Bess was staring at her. "Moreover, I don't understand your particular interest in Mr. Phillip Orleans. Although handsome, he seemed otherwise uninteresting to you. Why did you change your mind? Why have the boys follow him? Why would *you* follow him? He is no match for either of us when he is engaged to Kitty Tw—"

"Because he looks ever so like the Leaping Man."

Bess put her hand on Lillian's arm. "The Leaping Man, Lil?" she whispered. "Is that from one of your books? We should perhaps chat with Addie…"

Lillian stared into Bess's concerned blue eyes and sighed. Oh, what she wouldn't give to have a real partner, a real Dr. Watson to believe her. But she lived in a secret world where nothing was safe to share. They wouldn't believe the truth if she told them. She hardly believed the memory herself.

"Yes, Bess," she said. "It is a story from one of my books. I thought to have Miss Twamley paint a likeness to go with my favorite story, that is all. Phillip Orleans would make a fine protagonist. And perhaps he would sit for his betrothed." *Though I am interested in meeting the brother if he is truly taller and even more handsome…*

Bess looked doubtful, and Lillian knew her friend struggled with whether or not to pretend all was fine. "A painting of a character from a story?" she said at last. "I suppose that is acceptable. But you mustn't follow the man anywhere, Lil. It's simply not done—and it's not safe. Neither for you nor the Musketeers."

"When I choose to go, he will not know it is me. I will disguise myself as a boy. I will dress you in the same fashion, and even your father would not recognize you."

"Me!"

"All right, I will do it alone." *What am I putting her through? I'd be best alone, anyway. Perhaps I was meant to be always alone.*

"Do you think that thieves and cutthroats only accost girls?"

"I have a pistol, Bess."

"I try to forget that. Please don't mention it again. I've only been as far as the train station. I'm not allowed... I can't walk very far, and I don't have the money for..." She stared at nothing, twisted her handkerchief and wiggled her foot.

"You *can* walk far," Lillian said. "You choose not to, because you care more about the stares of strangers than fulfilling your desires. Please do not do this to yourself, Elisabeth. It is a crime against your own person. Even if you do not wish to follow Mr. Orleans you should—"

"I cannot go, and you will not go alone. I insist. Or...or, I will tell Thomas."

"Balderdash."

Bess held up her palm. "May I die a hatless old maid. I will tell him your plan. It is bad enough that you have tried to deceive us all, and often done so. You are far too clever. I know you ride that blasted steambike—"

"Steam-powered velocipede."

"—at *night*. I will love you no matter how you dress, no matter how many men you turn away, no matter how many invitations lay unopened on your desk. But you are asking too much. You are asking me not to care about you."

"I understand, Bess. But if you don't want me following anyone, will you at least help me uncover the truth about the Orleanses tonight? I do feel there is something odd about Phillip, and I cannot wait to meet the brother. I do so hope he is there. Perhaps you can speak with Kitty and learn all about him. How would that be? Then no one need head into the harbor district at midnight."

Bess's face brightened and she rose, clapping her hands together. "I would be thrilled to help in that manner!"

As she turned toward the door she hesitated a moment, but she did not turn back. Lillian knew her friend realized she'd been fooled again, that this was only the prelude of investigations yet to come.

She only prayed Bess would forgive her for the necessity of her actions and her lies.

Or, perhaps it was time to ask the doctor for help. Eventually she would lose everyone she cared about.

CHAPTER SEVEN

A Dangerous Woman

"So, Madam Pelosi, what brings you to Charm City? The oysters? The scum floating on the harbor? The fascinating society? I understand you are still practicing the dark arts to lure in your victims."

"Some things never change, George. Your wit hasn't improved. But it's good to see you, too."

George laughed and kissed the ridiculously attired would-be gypsy on the cheek. "Because it's about to pour, Phillip went to fetch Kitty and her dull friends in a cab. They should be here soon. So we have a moment to chat."

Annaluisa sat next to George and pulled his arm around her shoulders. "Let's talk about Kitty. This concerns me, Georgy. I have not seen such an arrangement ever end happily, have you? And Phillip shows a bit of disregard for his own kind by trusting her to stay silent."

"While I don't welcome the scrutiny of mortals, I believe that Kitty may be trusted. Her love for Phillip is strong."

"Obviously." Annaluisa paused. "To answer your initial question, I left New Orleans because the voodoo priestesses there are making it increasingly uncomfortable for our kind. While their magic is absurd, they do have a solid grasp of how to kill us. And you've been there enough to know how indiscreet the House can be—Jean's high opinion of his talents leaves him vulnerable, in my opinion. He should be more circumspect."

"I'm sure he has the power to take down any opposition—why should he care?"

"Your isolation has made you a bit naïve. If a handful of women have the knowledge to kill us, do you not think that knowledge will eventually spread? Our numbers are so great...how long before the legends of our kind are no longer legends to them, and the mortal masses declare war on our kind?"

"While I do love my fortune and my peace, I truly do not give a damn what happens to our kind. Let them destroy us all. It will not be for a while. Are you actually worried about this, Anna? Don't you sometimes wish for the end? Of course you do, why do I ask? You're nearly as old as I am. The thought of a few Caribbean ladies with wooden stakes hardly sends terror through my veins."

"No? Not even when they speak of a monster they call Madam Lucifer? It cannot be a coincidence."

George schooled his features so that no emotion would show, but her unexpected mention of Marie set his nerves sizzling. Could Annaluisa be trusted? She was a vampire, true, and an old friend, but Marie de Bourbon had tainted even his own mother. And Annaluisa had a decided appetite for intrigue and politics, making a habit of visiting as many houses as she could to maintain cordial relations. "Unlikely a coincidence, but the woman is in Europe. This tale of her in New Orleans smacks of folklore, fairytales to scare children."

"There is more. The rumor is that there is a price on your head, Georgy. A high one."

"What price? Who circulates this rumor? Who of any House lacks for riches? That is not motivation. Ridiculous." He forced himself to lower his tense shoulders. This was worse than he'd imagined.

"Not riches. Power. She's offered great power—her own blood, built of thousands of victims, including many, many vampires. No one is stronger."

"She is revolting, her practices anathema. But as vile as she is, even she wouldn't relinquish that power simply to see me suffer. I don't believe it. Although I sometimes wish I'd eaten more of my own kind to acquire that kind of force."

Annaluisa arched a brow to call him a liar. "Not even you have the stomach for that." George sighed in agreement.

"What is the saying about a woman scorned? You were lovers, were you not?"

"She was Phillip's wife. You have the wrong brother."

Annaluisa arched a heavily etched brow and fussed with her gold bangles. "Hardly. As I recall, you once left my bed to rush into hers. Did it never occur to you that she might love you? Something to do with that handsome face, perhaps?"

George rubbed his chin, weighing what she said, wondering if he could accept this accomplished trickster's words at face value. "I doubt it. I believe it is much simpler. She wouldn't be the first to come to loathe their maker—and her husband's maker." But he wondered. Had she loved him?

"Whatever the truth, she unquestionably wants your undoing."

"Where is she now?"

"Rumors have her in New Orleans, but I saw no evidence of it. You claim she is in Europe. Is it not like the woman to be talked about on more than one continent?" Annaluisa sighed. "There are too many of us, Georgy, don't you think? How many have you made? How many have they made? It's causing a political stir, alliances, betrayals. We have grown faster than the great new cities of this continent can absorb us. Soon there will be nowhere for you to cower in the shadows."

"It's terrible in Europe. I just came from London, and in the decade I've been away things have gotten very dicey."

"So you fled back to your brother's arms, as you've always been a lone wolf with no alliances."

"Yes, my fluffy white tail was singed by one of Madam Lucifer's jesters. He will make no more jokes for her, but there are hundreds, thousands perhaps, to take his place. No doubt she is displeased with me for removing one of her lieutenants." *Who to trust now? Phillip alone?*

"Ah. Marie de Bourbon does have the longest memory. Not too fond of me, either. Do you know that the last time I saw her she accused me of stealing a rather enormous emerald from her? At least three hundred years ago!"

"No doubt you did."

"Of course. But my point is that she remembered." Annaluisa shook her head sadly. "So, back to Kitty. This is a fairly intolerable situation, as I adore Phillip. Fortunately there is no governing House in Baltimore, or they would have his head. A human lover who knows so much…"

George rubbed at his chin. "Haven't we all gone through a spell of wanting a normal life and trying to make it happen? That is what's at play here. She knows and yet she loves him."

"What does she know, exactly? Phillip swore that she doesn't know about me but that the jig is up for you. How does that make you feel? If you killed or turned her, Georgy, it would be as if you are no longer brothers, and I know that despite your differences he loves you and you love him. You must realize what a precarious thing this is. You pretend to be ambivalent about your relationship with Phillip, but I know the truth."

"I do realize. Everything. Of course." *You have no idea. But I need him.*

"Ah, I hear a carriage. Let me go apply more paint so that I may play my role. One of the guests is the child of a friend. I'm feeling generous. She needs a bit of gypsy magic to sooth her wounded soul, although she doesn't realize it."

George glanced up. "Oh, anyone I know?"

74

"Shush, here they come. Straighten your necktie, Georgy, and join your man at the door. Be a good host, or Kitty will call in the voodoo priestesses."

"More likely to call in her Irish priests, Annaluisa," he called after her as she scurried upstairs.

The not-so-dulcet tones of Etta and Agnes Langhan, their wealthy spinster neighbors, made George cringe as he joined his butler at the door. "Phillip will pay for this, Jameson. The Langhan sisters?"

"Indeed, sir. We must steel ourselves for the evening. Hopefully the piano has not also fallen out of tune."

George patted Jameson's back and then slipped him a ten-dollar note. The butler surely earned more than the average banker in Baltimore, but that seemed the price of secrecy. That and…certain other precautions. No vampire would work as a butler, at least not for very long. And so, mortals. Jameson had lasted longer than any before him.

Plastering a smile on his face, the one that Phillip often called his crocodile grin, George politely ushered in the rotund duo. The Langhan sisters were the pinnacle of Baltimore society, avid art collectors, friends of poets and novelists, and prone to chatter in French so poorly accented it made George's teeth ache. Behind them, Phillip ushered Kitty on one arm and a rather ordinary plump blonde morsel on his other. On another night she would be his mark for an evening snack, despite her unattractive limp. Tonight he would treat her as though anything she uttered fascinated him.

He was about to close the door behind them when he realized the party was not yet complete. A tall, slender woman had her back to him and seemed fascinated with something on the ground outside. He laughed as she knelt on all fours, pulled a matchbox from her bag and lit a match, and ran her hand along the wet grass and mud fronting the house.

"Perhaps she'll hold that position for me," he muttered, taking in her slender waist, full bottom, and breasts straining against her gown. *A much better morsel!*

The blonde woman suddenly squealed and scurried past George, rushing out and back to the other's side, pulling at her sleeve and whispering into her ear. She seemed upset.

"Why, Phillip," George said, feeling his brother's presence beside him, "what on earth is your guest up to?"

Phillip joined him in the doorway and shrugged. "How peculiar. You two should hit it off." He lowered his voice and whispered, "Be nice. Perhaps she is not quite right."

The woman stood, brushed off her dress, and turned to the house. George forgot to breathe for a moment, and by the look on her face, so did the object of his attention.

"Why, she's really as beautiful as I remembered."

Phillip elbowed him. "You know her?"

She stood naked in a window and watched me flee my victim's bedroom. "Oh, I'm mistaken. She looks like someone else."

The blonde seemed flustered as she pulled her friend up the stairs, the latter walking slowly as if in a trance. Yes, she might be a little daft, George decided. But when she passed by him, she cast a quick glance at his face and pretended to smile.

Pretended? His heart quickened, fear and excitement warring within. Did she truly remember him? It had been dark and misty. He'd been disguised. Well, honestly, he'd been drunk on fresh blood and wasn't sure.

They assembled in the parlor and Kitty made the introductions. The blonde…he forgot her name the moment it was mentioned. The brunette was Lillian Holmes, of the Federal Hill neighborhood. That would put her in the right location.

The blonde spoke in a rush. "Why, please excuse Lillian. She dropped her ring upon exiting the carriage and knelt to look for it. Isn't that right, Lil?"

Lillian stared straight on at George for the first time, a hint of a smile pulling her lip up on one side. She narrowed her eyes, and although she fussed with her bag, she never broke that stare. "That is quite right, Bess. So lucky that I found exactly what I was looking for. One can never be quite certain in the dark, but some objects are not easily mistaken."

A deep sense of satisfaction and longing sang through George's veins. A formidable opponent, this Lillian Holmes seemed. All the sweeter to be brought to her knees, literally and figuratively.

The guests were silent, watching him and Lillian as if they didn't know what sporting event was about to commence but knowing a competition when they saw one. Yes, he would give her a good run. Here was a mortal woman worth his time, at least for a short while. She would be the amusement to help take his mind off a far less attractive and deadlier foe.

CHAPTER EIGHT

In the lion's den.

Lillian forced her gaze away from the Leaping Man. How could it be chance? Surely some nefarious plot was unraveling before her eyes, although she was no longer looking on from a safe distance. No, she sat within a few feet of an exquisite, evil murderer.

She turned and withdrew from her bag one of the pills the good doctor has given her, feigning a touch of her handkerchief upon her neck. But at a snicker from her right, she looked up. He'd seen her. Actually, he hadn't taken his gaze off of her, even though his eyes seemed half-closed.

Lillian had felt herself be undressed by a man's gaze before, but this was undressing down to the bone. His dark eyes seemed to deepen in color as she met his gaze. Did he breathe? He seemed carved of pale stone, his thick raven hair accentuating the pallor. It should have repulsed her, but she stared transfixed by his...spell? Yes, it was as if he cast a spell on her.

This medicine. Am I imagining things?

She forced herself to sit straight and to hold her hands still rather than reach for Bess's and flee the house immediately. Uncle would not flee. He would stay and play cat and mouse with his prey, learning more than the criminal meant to reveal. But Bess was no Watson, and Lillian gulped down the horrible thought that she might be putting her friend in danger as well.

She forced a bit of a smile at the sisters Langhan, bedecked in many yards of black and burgundy silk and bantering back and forth

78

about a burgeoning French style of painting. What to do? These women were at risk also, were they not? Or were they part of a gang of murderers, however unlikely it seemed?

Kitty Twamley sat nearby, smiling merrily, clearly enjoying the night already, clearly happy to be at a social event. How many events like this had the young woman longed for but never been invited to? Like Bess, Lillian realized. No doubt she'd been uplifted in station by association with her betrothed. Still, she seemed innocent enough. Not part of a pack of murderers.

Lillian's head swam, and her hand shook as she reached for another pill. Damnation, but they were so weak compared to Mrs. Winslow's remedy! How could she be so uncertain? She'd studied, prepared as well as any detective could. But she was a fool. *You have no real training. Charlatan, egotistical charlatan. Now what?*

She resolved to wait.

Her limbs grew heavy, and a bit of her tension drained away as she sipped at her cordial and the pills soothed her nerves. *You always have your pistol,* she reminded herself. They could stay a while, collect some data and then call directly on Constable Johnnie Moran, who was likely dining at her home right this moment. She had arranged a pleasant dinner for him and Aileen to take the place of this engagement.

"Pride goeth before the fall."

"Excuse me, Miss Holmes?" The Leaping Man leaned forward, a different intensity in his stare now. He was no longer undressing her with his eyes but trying to read her thoughts, and it seemed as if she were back in Dr. Schneider's office. The scrutiny made her skin burn and her heart quicken.

"Did I say something, Mr. Orleans?" God, had she actually spoken aloud?

"Please do call me George. I believe you quoted a famous saying about pride. I concur, of course. I've often told dear Phillip here the same thing. He, however, insists I am the more prideful of the two of us."

"That does not surprise me. You are the older brother, it seems? Are there any more in the family?"

"Alas, only us. I hope that does not disappoint."

"Hardly. I do not believe Baltimore could contain more than two Orleans siblings."

The Leaping Man cocked his head to the side, and the nervous game relaxed for a moment as he seemed to see her anew. "And what makes you say that?"

"You both fill the room somehow." Her head began to throb, and she set down her glass. How many pills had she taken?

"Are you all right, Lil? You're a bit pale." Bess had linked arms with her and whispered into her ear.

"As pale as Mr. Orleans?" Lillian whispered, wondering if her friend noticed how unnatural both brothers seemed. "Yes, quite all right. A glass of water might be welcome."

George heard her and signaled to the butler, who quickly returned with the requested beverage. She sipped, and the cacophony of voices faded into the background.

A few deep, cleansing breaths and she turned back to George, whose appeal shocked her anew. "Have you been in Baltimore long, Mr. Orleans?"

"Do you dislike the name George? I would change it for you—"

"Your answer, George?"

He quirked a brow and sharply sat up. Lillian knew he must think her quite insane, first seeing her examine the soil outside his house to compare it to that found on her neighbor's fire escape, and now to appear so fragile of constitution and so sharp of tongue...

Why did she care what a cutthroat thought, no matter how handsome and extraordinary? *Here is your Moriarity. You wanted one. Do not lose sight of that.*

She didn't get her answer from George, as Madam Annaluisa Pelosi swept down the staircase in a swirl of scarves and bangles, leaving a trail of exotic scents in her wake. Lillian groaned, having forgotten the entertainment portion of the evening. What an annoying distraction.

As the guests greeted Annaluisa, she warded them off with a dramatic flourish of her hand and drew a scarf across her face. Then she beckoned to a round table at the far end of the room.

"Oh, a séance?" Bess breathed out excitedly. Everyone bustled toward the table but Lillian and George.

He stood and extended his hand to help her up, but she was frozen, turned to stone by his intense stare, which failed to be softened by his smirk. "I believe we are required to join…although I sense you have no more interest than I in the spirit world. Perhaps you would prefer to steal away?"

"In your company? I believe I would prefer the company of spirits."

He laughed openly, and Lillian felt herself smile against her will. How could this handsome, intelligent man be the Leaping Man? And yet, he must be. Then he is the worst kind of evil, for he is charming, she reminded herself. Not in the false way her fortune-hunting suitors were charming. Not the studied charm of society. No, this man had depth and perhaps a bit of sorrow or pain that made him endearing despite his reprehensible actions.

She took his hand, and despite the coldness emanating from it her body warmed at the contact. Again a bit dizzy, she did need to rely on his steadying arm.

They walked to join the other guests, and as they did she tried to secure more data. "George, you never answered. How long have you been in Baltimore? Where are you from?"

"A good long time, and France. Would you answer the same?"

"You have no accent that I can detect. I have been here all my life. Although my family—that is, my uncles—live in England."

And now he knows more about you than you do about him. You have met your match, Lillian Holmes. Or worse. There is real evil in the world, Mr. Conan Doyle had written. And I am holding Evil's arm, she thought.

They took the only two spots left at the table, George to her right and Phillip to her left. Lillian barely cared about looking for the medium's tricks, which might be an amusing challenge on another evening. No, she had to confirm her suspicions about George. Had he known the Mayor? Was he in the employ of a political enemy? But what of her young neighbor? Who could possibly want the death of an ordinary, innocent boy?

George sat too close. He studied her without looking at her, and the hairs on her arms bristled at the sensation.

Lillian caught the most fleeting contact between George and Annaluisa as she instructed her guests to hold hands atop the table. What was their connection? They certainly had met before this evening. Was the medium a partner in some awful plot? Lillian cast her gaze about the room, finding only the butler lurking in the shadows and the other guests showing varying degrees of interest or amusement.

You have your pistol. But now she would have to release the hands of the Orleans brothers to fetch it from the bag in her lap.

The séance proceeded as Lillian expected, with the snuffing of most of the candles in the room, chanting and swaying from Madam Pelosi, and a bit of snickering from the Langhan sisters. Their mirth ceased when the medium announced the arrival of their first otherworldly guest.

"Who is this? A famous artist, he claims. A Monsieur Eugene Delacroix?"

"Oh! We have one of his works!" Etta Langhan said to her sister, who nodded. "Could he want to speak to us?"

"Yeeeeeessssss… he would like to thank you and implores you to continue your patronage of artists like the talented Miss Twamley."

"Gracious!" Kitty exclaimed.

Lillian resisted sighing loudly.

George leaned behind Lillian toward his brother and whispered in French, "Isn't that the chap you commissioned to paint a mural when you were on the throne? Had him locked up for some reason?"

"Quiet, you idiot," Phillip retorted in the same language.

Throne? What on earth had George meant? The artist had been dead for decades in any case. Lillian resisted a reply in French to show them she had heard. *No, do not play all of your cards now. Perhaps they will continue their conversation.*

The spirits evidently lined up to speak through Madam Pelosi, as there was a communication for each person at the table: Kitty's brother Patrick was happy after his illness and reunited with his parents, which made her brush a tear from her cheek; Agnes Langhan would make a great scientific discovery, according to her former colleague; Bess's grandmother assured her of an unexpected treasure; and Phillip and George's father was sorely disappointed in them, urging them to apply themselves more. The last elicited a howl of glee from the pair, making it clear that Annaluisa was in on the joke with them.

Lillian pushed down a lump in her throat. Thank God, no message for her. The medium no doubt understood she was too intelligent to fall for such a crude game. *But… But what, Lil? Who would you hear from, even if it were possible? Your parents would not reveal themselves in life, much less in death.*

Bess, trying to be helpful, glanced at her, and Lillian shook her intention off with a glare.

"The spirit world has not ignored your friend, Miss Wheeler." Annaluisa moaned and swayed again, eyes closed.

As if he read her dread, George squeezed Lillian's hand gently and leaned close. "You do understand that this is a game? Your blood pounds through your veins at a startling rate. Please, do not be afraid."

"Of course not." But fear gripped at her chest, fear of the man who tried to calm her, fear of the woman who tried to trick her, fear at the sensations swirling in her head, through her body. Another pill would help, but it was too late for that.

"Quiet! She approaches!" Annaluisa scolded. And Lillian knew that once again she would speak of her mother, a woman with no name, no heart, no connection to her life after the moment of giving birth. It was a low, low trick to play on one's emotions. Was the Leaping Man in on the ruse? Were the two trying to break her spirit, her mind?

"No!" Lillian pulled away from the men and stood. Despite the longing for answers, the horrid gaping hole in her chest, the years of wondering and wanting, she would not be a pawn in a parlor game.

Madam Pelosi opened her eyes. "Oh, my dear, please, I can tell you about her."

"You cannot, and I will not pretend that you can."

George rose and supported her arm, and despite all rational thought Lillian welcomed the comfort. "We will respect Miss Holmes's wishes. Shall we move to the living room, Lillian? I tire of this myself."

She glanced into his dark eyes and saw what she never expected: sincerity. Why would a murderer want to give her comfort?

"No," she said, "I'm afraid it is time for me to depart. I am getting one of my headaches." Though, Bess would not want to depart. She could not leave her friend behind amongst these strange creatures.

Kitty looked on the verge of tears as she approached. "I am sorry you do not feel well, Miss Holmes. Did the séance upset you? Perhaps on another evening—?"

"I have had a wonderful time, Miss Twamley. You are a great hostess. I simply have not been at my best today. I hope that one day soon you will visit my home."

Kitty seemed relieved by the lie. Lillian waited by the door as goodbyes were said. Surprising her, Bess linked arms with her and reluctantly pulled her across the threshold and down the stairs, obviously overcoming her desire to stay in order to keep Lillian out of mischief. It was likely a wise move. Lillian looked back to find George Orleans standing on the porch, arms folded, head tilted, smiling curiously. He inclined his head slightly before she turned, and she could feel his stare burn into her back as she and Bess walked home.

After a few deep breaths her hands had nearly stopped shaking and she reached into her bag for a pill.

"Lil! What are you taking? You are not yourself at all tonight!"

"Nonsense. I am quite myself. Who else would I be?"

"Hm." Bess clearly did not know how to respond to that. "Kitty is nice, don't you think? I hope to see her again." She paused. "It is a strange household, though. I think, Lillian, you are influencing me finally. I believe Madam Pelosi is a charlatan."

"I thought it a bit dense for her to expect your living grandmothers to speak to you from beyond the grave. She did no research. And the Orleans brothers, Bess?"

"Must I look past their manly beauty? Then, yes, they are…different somehow."

"Yes, Bess. They are different. The game is afoot."

"You have said that before. I have no idea what that means."

"You will."

*****

Rain came that evening, but it did not clear the city of heat. Lillian heard the chatter of the Musketeers as they bid Constable Moran goodnight and accompanied Aileen to their new quarters on the third floor. Lillian listened to ensure Abraham Lincoln did not accompany them, and then turned back to her journal.

Shocked that her hand still quivered, she put down her pen and withdrew her pistol from her desk drawer. Her bottle of medicine, nearly empty, rattled in the drawer, and she stared at it while thinking about George Orleans.

Why had she ignored Constable Johnnie Moran and gone to her room without mentioning the fact that she had sat in the home of the Leaping Man, the murderer of Baltimore's mayor, of a young neighbor, and God only knew how many others? Certainly it wasn't the man's charm that saved him, although he *was* charming in some unholy fashion she couldn't identify. Did she truly intend to prove her case first, and report her findings to Scotland Yard? *Scotland Yard, Lillian?* No, the Baltimore city precinct.

She sat at her desk and drank the blue bottle empty. Tomorrow she would begin Dr. Schneider's course of slow weaning; that would be the time to stop.

Fury swept through her suddenly, and Lillian threw the bottle into the cold fireplace. If only Madam Pelosi *could* speak to the dead, tell her who she was, why she was, what she was to do with her life! Only the Leaping Man seemed the least interested in guarding her from the charlatan. He had seemed to understand her pain somehow. Or was that wishful thinking? No one understood. Well, perhaps Dr. Schneider did, but she feared him as much as the Leaping Man. One could imprison her and one could kill her. There was no one to trust. Perhaps Addie and Thomas had already sided fully with the Jackal.

The city was calling to her through the open window. The bay. Release. She glanced out to look for the Leaping Man before yelling at the city and slamming the window shut.

"Holmes! You aren't making sense," she said aloud.

Uncle had known times like this, when he was besieged by the Melancholies. He'd take up his violin or shut himself away for days. She had no violin, and the Jackal would not let her hide. Perhaps it would be best if the Leaping Man killed her and hopped off her balcony, carrying away her pain into the night. A profound hurt welled up in her chest and she fell to her knees, sobbing for the losses of people and promises she'd never know.

After some minutes, exhausted, she crawled into bed, some of the tension of her body relieved by her weeping. She would go to sleep, and in the morning, all would feel brighter. "The best bridge between despair and hope is a good night's sleep," Addie was fond of saying.

Casting her evening dress aside, Lillian lay on the bed in her chemise and bloomers, and tucked her pistol under her pillow. She lost track of the chimes of the clock tower before it struck its final note.

CHAPTER NINE

Desperate times and desperate measures.

George knew his brooding annoyed Phillip to no end. No, that wasn't quite right. It worried his brother, and the worry would start to annoy him and wear him down. But this steady ethical diet of the dangerous men of Baltimore had soured his temperament. Still, Phillip was coming to appreciate his efforts at walking the straight and narrow, no doubt doubly so since Kitty eyed him like a hawk.

He had to get out alone or go mad. And he had a terrible predicament on his hands.

"Are you ready?" Phillip asked as he threw on his overcoat.

"I don't want to hunt tonight. I'll keep Kitty company. Where is she?"

"In my bed and you well know it. You've bedded and eaten too many of my women already."

"You wound me sometimes, Phillip. Really, I do have feelings."

"I'm too tired for your jokes."

"Is Kitty going to stay here at the house before you get married? It will elicit censure in the neighborhood. And it puts a severe damper on things for me."

"Things you should not be at in the first place. It's late. She was tired."

"Yes, that's the reason. Oh, don't look at me like that. I'm jealous of your lovely little romance and you've caught me. Now be a good boy and run along, leave me with my brooding and my pipe."

Phillip didn't leave but seemed to weigh the merits of an argument in advance. "Then, you won't go out tonight?"

"I don't think so. You can't watch me every moment, keep me prisoner here! Must I promise?"

"Yes, I think you must. And you must promise not to harm Kitty, for all that your promises are worth."

George clasped his hands over his heart solemnly. "I will not harm an innocent mortal this evening. You really are too much."

"Go to hell," Phillip called over his shoulder as he left.

"Yes, well, who knows about that? One would have to believe in a God for there to be a heaven and hell. These things are the least of my worries."

Peace, blessed solitude. Madam Pelosi was back to her hotel, the yapping Langhans back to their mansion, Kitty asleep, Phillip gone. The blonde—what was her name?—no doubt dreaming of a handsome suitor.

And Lillian Holmes. What of that enigmatic beauty? She'd recognized him. Still, she'd faced him head-on, chin high, eyes scanning his for guilt. What he wouldn't give to have her back in the house, clutching his hand in mixed horror and excitement. Her pounding heart had nearly drowned out the voices around them. Her beautiful face, delicious figure, and extraordinary intellect—despite something muddling her mind—made him anxious for a few moments alone to fantasize about a sexual liaison with her.

So, she thought him a murderer. *Well, you are, George.* But she'd never come to know the truth of his existence. How could she? Annaluisa had told him she didn't even know her own heritage, hadn't spent more than a month with her mother before the woman became a victim of Madam Lucifer. Orphaned without knowing why. Perhaps she had indeed gone daft as Phillip suggested. She acted curiously enough.

Annaluisa had thought a bit of the tale might help Lillian gain confidence, soften the blow of being alone in the world. George had convinced her that the woman was driven enough to try to track down the truth—which was ugly indeed—and intelligent enough to succeed. Mother was a vampire living in London, not killed but turned by Madam Lucifer. She'd killed Father. Annaluisa had finally conceded to silence after talking it through, agreeing that Lillian seemed likely to pursue the facts to their inevitable deadly end.

But, what was he to do about her? Why weren't the police at the door right now if she intended to turn him in for killing her neighbor? Dimwitted, immoral, lazy…none of that fit her. So she was waiting for something, planning something beyond his understanding. But what? And could he allow it to happen?

If he killed her, Phillip would recognize his hand in the murder. *And I don't want to kill her. Not yet.*

Why, I'd actually like to spend some time with her, he realized in wonder. When was the last time he felt that way about a mortal? Far past the decades when he longed for a normal life, it was something of an unwelcome anomaly.

George brushed aside his thoughts and put down his pipe, knowing what he must do. But as he left the Orleans home, he wondered if he'd ever be welcome to enter again. If Phillip would speak to him again. His only ally.

Well, he'd have to fix that and amass a following. If Marie de Bourbon had done so, he surely could. With his looks, charm, and hunger, he could have his own House in Baltimore, dull as the city was. Perhaps he'd start with the lovely Miss Holmes.

Invigorated, George nodded to the usual characters who shared the night with him as he walked towards Federal Hill: a carriage driver hoping for a final customer; a young man hurrying home on unsteady legs, no doubt after some raucous outing; a few servants playing dice and drinking. Soon he stood in the alleyway beneath the house where his last "murder" occurred and peered up at Lillian Holmes's balcony. There was no God to intervene on his behalf, and so he would have to kill her or turn her. His fervor cooled now that he was close to his goal, he half wished the situation were reversed. But tired, so tired of his life, he nonetheless found the energy to leap to her window.

George peered into the room carefully, lest she be up and about. But no, even in the dim light of the moon he saw her tall figure stretched out on the bed in filmy white as if she were on her funeral bier. The sight stirred so much in him: lust, for both the sexual beauty and her blood; sorrow, for what he would no doubt need to do to her; fear, for she made him loathe himself and he didn't like that.

He stepped across the sill into the room, still unsure of what exactly he would do but knowing he must act to save himself, to sate himself. Unlike Phillip, he wouldn't indulge in longing for a normal life, for romance and companionship. But oh, wouldn't she be a companion? So odd, this beauty. So strong and fragile at the same time. Annaluisa had said her mother was a beauty as well, and of course was one still. But George was certain the mother couldn't have the spirit or intellect of Lillian Holmes.

Damnation, this is cruel. I don't want to kill her, he thought. If I don't, I will have to flee Baltimore, for she might be wise enough to uncover the truth. And then he'd be alone again against Madam Lucifer. He knew what she'd been up to in the mud of his front lawn. He knew she had the strength and wit to do verbal battle with him, despite knowing him to be a murderer. What would she do if she knew the bitter truth? Revile him more, for certain. No, she would turn him in. She must be stopped.

But perhaps he could leave her be, take Phillip's suggestion and find a spot of boring solitude, hide away like the refugee he was. Alone, yes, but what else was new? Phillip had tried to love him for years and seemed nearly ready to give up. Perhaps those days of trying were finally over. They certainly would be if he learned of George slaying this beautiful girl in her bed.

Lillian stirred a bit and rolled onto her side. George groaned as the play of moonlight on her long legs, hips and breasts made his body tingle in anticipation of all she might offer both man and vampire. He noticed perspiration gleaming on her pale skin as he got closer. The night wasn't that hot; was she ill? No matter, even if she had the plague, it wouldn't kill him. He'd learned that firsthand a few centuries earlier.

He knelt beside her and lightly brushed her damp raven-dark hair away from her neck. The sound of her coursing blood screamed at him from her veins, but he watched her for a moment while his sadness for her—for himself—made him curse. *Thank God no one can see me so weak.*

She moaned and threw her arm over her head. Ah, a dream. Did she dream of him? Or was it a nightmare of him? He leaned in close to her neck, the pounding through her arteries practically deafening, matching the beat of his own black heart. Had he ever felt such a bloodlust? Not since the early days. He would have her, every drop of her.

To his shock, her eyes shot open, expressionless. As if he belonged there, she stared at him and let out a deep breath. Then she closed her eyes again, and he wondered if she were indeed ill, but her breathing steadied and she fell asleep again.

His lust driving him insane, he inched his way onto the bed and lay alongside her, struggling against touching the swell of her breasts, her collarbone, her neck. He might murder, but he would not rape. She rolled to her side and moaned in her sleep, and he pressed himself along the soft length of her until his pulse beat in concert with hers. *Here is my match,* he heard himself think. Would she mind so much if he touched her before she died?

She moaned when he ran his hand along her hip and then up her torso to brush against the soft underside of her bosom. Then she took in a quick breath and reopened her eyes.

"Am I dreaming?" she slurred in a whisper. It broke his heart, for she sounded so lonely.

"Yes, my mortal queen, you are asleep." He brushed her eyelids closed and kissed her lips gently, wondering which would be the harsher sentence for her, death or undeath. How much better he understood Phillip now.

She forced her bleary eyes open and stared into his. "You will take me before killing me?"

His heart dropped. Awake, then, and aware of her awful predicament.

"No, I will not. I am a monster, but even I would not do that."

"But you will kill me?"

"Kiss me, Lillian."

He heard the desperation in his own voice and choked back the pain rising in his chest. She did kiss him, but then whispered against his cheek, "Why must you kill? Tell me that at least?"

"I kill to live. I am *vampyr*."

But she didn't seem to hear him, as she closed her eyes and faded back into her stupor.

Get it over with.

George pressed his torso against hers, pinning her to the bed, and he pushed her chin to the side, exposing her lovely pale neck. Then, "I hate you, Mother," he said before he sank his teeth into Lillian's flesh.

He muffled her cry with his hand as the first taste of her rushed through him. Suddenly disoriented, head throbbing in pain, he pulled back for a moment. What had she taken? How did she endure such vile potions? But they would not stop him from feeding. He leaned in to drink fully, to send her into a dreamless, painless sleep.

Was it the potions intoxicating him? Her blood at once sated and aroused him as none had done since his first meal, the blood of his own mother. That had made him die and be reborn at the same time. So felt the blood of Lillian Holmes. Death and life. Why would this fragile mortal have such power? What pull she had on his soul! No, he had no soul—

He heard a loud pop and felt a burn in his chest.

"I do not think you will kill me tonight," she hissed, and pushed him away.

"God, you fool!" Blood seeped through his shirt and fell in droplets onto her nightclothes.

"Who is the fool, sir?"

The sting of the bullet faded quickly and the blood flow ceased, but Lillian still aimed her pistol at him. Blood dripped from her neck, and he nearly lost sense as hunger overwhelmed him.

"You really should stop indulging that drug habit," he drawled. "Your blood is quite tainted. It will kill you, you know."

She shot him again, and he winced. But the noise was worse than the pain. The house came to life with sounds of women and children shouting and opening doors. Perhaps they had not recognized the first noise as a shot when it rang out.

George pulled a small knife from his pocket, dragged it across his bloodied chest and dropped it on the floor. Another suicide—but this time a failed attempt, the police would conclude. They would surely not believe whatever report Lillian gave of him. He could likely depend upon that much, given her drugged state.

Her eyes burned with fear and her hand shook, but she aimed her pistol steady as the clamor grew in the hallway. She would soon have reinforcements.

"No time for goodbyes, Lillian. I do hope we meet again."

"Have no fear! I will visit you in prison or see you in hell!"

George fled to the balcony, jumped down into the alley, and flew from the neighborhood.

Oddly, he chuckled a bit as he fled, wondering if he knew anyone interesting in Africa or the Orient. For now he had one choice: to go far enough away that Madam Lucifer, Phillip, Kitty, and the lovely Lillian Holmes would never find him. But that didn't remove his strange happiness that he'd been unable to kill her.

"I am truly the most unlucky man ever born," he muttered as he entered his home through the back door. And he was. Phillip was waiting for him, arms crossed and eyebrow raised, ready for a fight.

"I hope you are satisfied. Because of you I hunted in the filthy alleyways tonight and was shot. Twice! I didn't even get a taste before the police whistles sounded." His thoughts still on Lillian, George fumbled a bit with his lies, but Phillip's stern expression disappeared.

"I told you to go with me. I feared that… Never mind. I'm off to bed. Kitty no doubt has waited up for me."

"Phillip?"

His brother had started up the stairs. He turned and frowned.

"You're lucky to have Kitty. And you deserve that happiness. You were always a good man."

"Going soft on me, George, or do you need something again?"

"No, nothing like that."

His brother shook his head and headed up to the solace of his beloved's arms.

George picked up his pipe and sat, taking a moment to rest in case the police came to the front door. He rather doubted anyone would believe Lillian's story, but he'd been surprised before in his long lifetime. He hoped his brother would miss him if that happened, just a little bit. But he doubted it. He'd earned Phillip's disdain over so many years of flip remarks and broken promises. Perhaps after another fifty years or so, circumstances would shift and they could be together again.

***

"Stop it!" Lillian shouted, unable to stand the chaos. Her head threatened to explode, and the pain in her neck matched that of her heart. How had she suffered this neck wound? He'd leaned in to kiss her...

No. She simply wanted a moment to take in the truth of her attack, whatever that truth was. A *vampire*? Had George Orleans claimed to be a vampire? Then he was as mad as he was evil. Perhaps she could almost forgive him if he were mad, if he had no control over his actions. What she really wanted was for him not to be the murderer.

If he meant to slit her throat with that knife, he'd surely have succeeded. And she'd felt no pain as she fumbled for the pistol under her pillow. But perhaps the pills were to blame for that.

"I must stop the blood flow from this wound," Addie chastised with a shaky voice as she pressed the corner of the light blanket to Lillian's neck. "Oh, Lil. How did we let it get this bad? This is my fault. I should have..." She shook her head, devastated.

"How is it your fault, Addie? That does not make sense."

"Aileen, take the boys away. All will be fine," Thomas ordered.

The maid was as white as a ghost and tried to block her brothers' view of the scene. "Is Lil going to be all right?" she cried, the boys cried. Everyone but Lillian was crying.

"Send the boys to fetch Dr. Schneider. Go!" Thomas shoed them off and closed the bedroom door. He picked up George's knife from the floor and choked back a sob as he wiped the blood with a handkerchief.

"There, Lillian," Addie cooed in a tone she hadn't used in years. "The doctor will sew up this wound and you'll be fine. Now, give that pistol to Thomas."

Lillian looked at the pistol, having forgotten that she still held it, and dropped it onto the bed. "It didn't kill him. Two shots to the chest didn't kill him." How could that be? "He said he was a vampire. He said he killed so that he could live."

Addie gasped and held her hand over her mouth.

Thomas sat on the bed and put his arm around his sister's shoulder. "Who are you talking about, Lil?" he asked gently.

"My attacker, of course. The Leaping Man." *He caressed me, and it felt wonderful for a moment. He did so only so he could kill me as I slept. Or am I imagining that he wanted to kill me? He didn't harm me, did he? He kissed me. No, my neck, my neck is wounded.*

Addie and Thomas exchanged a look and Lillian's heart raced. *Oh, no!* What unimaginable events! Now the Jackal would swoop in and demand her rehabilitation. They would take her pistol, they would take her freedom. She pushed down a voice at the edge of her mind that wondered if they wouldn't be right to do so. Her heart sank. Hadn't she been tracking a dangerous man? Hadn't he come to her door? What if he'd hurt Aileen or one of the children? This was all so much easier in the stories!

"He came in from the balcony," she hurried to say. "You see, I must have left the window open. I was so tired and it was so hot."

"Your eyes look wild, dear. Please calm yourself and lie back down."

"Did you hear me? He came through the window while I slept, kissed me, and then somehow…we must have struggled, for I wounded my neck. I shot him twice but he fled back through the window!"

Thomas glanced at the knife.

Oh, God, help me! "No, Thomas! That is *his* knife, and that is not my blood on it. Don't you see? The mayor, the boy, and now me? They were not suicides. How could you think I would do such a thing? Why would I shoot my pistol? Is my neck sliced?" She pushed Addie's hand away and felt at her flesh. "No, these are small marks…"

"Did you use the tip of the knife, Lil?"

"I did not use the knife!"

"Who is this Leaping Man, Lillian? Is that his name?"

"Of course that is not his name! Oh, please, you must listen to me! I can show you in my journal, the night he leapt from the balcony after murdering the boy…"

The Adencourts' stares were sad and incredulous. Lillian lay back on the bed and wept, her shock now giving way to a new fear. The people she loved most in the world thought her lost. Bess would, too. Dr. Schneider… He was her only hope—unless somehow she could find George Orleans and capture him, force him to tell the truth.

Oh, how would I convince him? No one would believe me! If I accuse a wealthy gentleman of attacking me and then leaping two stories to the ground they will lock me away. No one will believe me. No one.

"The bleeding has slowed. Lie still while I tie a cloth to it, Lil. The doctor will be here shortly. Rest now. Everything will be fine."

Stop saying that! Nothing is fine! A murderer is running loose in the city, and no one will listen to me.

"Yes, you are right," she forced herself to say. "I feel a bit better. Can I have a little privacy now before Dr. Schneider arrives?"

Thomas and Addie looked at one another and then nodded. But Thomas took the pistol, the knife, and a letter opener on her desk, while Addie rifled through her drawers, evidently not for the first time. Thomas locked the window and lowered the lamp. They left her in peace, then, but not until after Addie picked Lillian's purse from the dresser and took it with her. And with that purse, Lillian's only solace, the little weak pills.

"So be it, I need a clear head now." But her body ached and her hands shook.

Who would help her? Watson! Bess knew her methods, had heard her mention the Leaping Man, even thought the Orleans household to be odd. With a glimmer of hope, Lillian sat at her desk and wrote a long note. She folded it into a tiny parcel and waited for the visit she knew would come.

When the maid finally tapped at her door, Lillian sighed in relief. "Quick. Come in, Aileen!"

"Are you all right, Miss? I'm so worried for you."

"Listen, Aileen, I do not have time to explain it all. You must trust me and put aside your worries for me."

"I've always trusted you, Miss."

Lillian held Aileen by the shoulders and stared deep into her bloodshot eyes. "Whatever anyone says, Aileen, I swear by my Maker that I am not insane, at least not about tonight's events. But I do need your assistance." She shoved the note to Bess into the maid's hands. "As first light, you must go to Miss Wheeler and give her this. Tell her nothing of what transpired tonight. Simply give this to her. Can you do that?"

"Of course, Miss. I can go now if you like. Should I see Johnnie as well? He might be able to help, too."

"Constable Moran can read, can he not?"

Aileen nodded.

"Then promise you will not give this to him. Do as I say. Only Miss Wheeler should read this."

"Aye, I will do as you say." Aileen hugged Lillian and pressed a kiss to her cheek. "If you are running away for some reason, Miss, please know that I love you, and I always will, no matter what you've done."

"Running away? Why, no, I'm not running away." But the maid's words made her pause. *Should I flee? Where on earth would I go? Perhaps that is what I must do. But then the murderer will go free, continue to destroy life.*

"Good night then, Miss."

Aileen slipped out, and Lillian whispered to the closed door, "I love you, too, Aileen. And the boys. I should have done more for you earlier."

CHAPTER TEN

A guilty conscience.

George woke, clothes bloody, hair disheveled, wondering what could possibly have taken Lillian so long to report him, or if his plan to cover his attack had truly worked. His heart dropped at the thought that she might have died from her neck wound.

No, it hadn't been that deep, he hadn't drunk much, and she'd been in full charge of her senses when he left. The entire house had stirred, and no doubt they had come to her aid. Could she actually want him to remain free? He doubted a few kisses had swayed her. She continued to be an enigma.

It was morning. George heard Phillip and Kitty stirring upstairs, and he rushed to clean up and plan his next step. God, what he wouldn't give to stay here. But Lillian would make that impossible. He might go back and kill her this evening, but she would likely be guarded. And she still had that damned pistol that could make a racket.

As he finished shaving in his bathroom, he heard a conversation in the foyer downstairs. Who would be calling so early? Had Lillian finally visited the police? No, the voice was female, and familiar.

He tiptoed down a few of the stairs and saw the blonde morsel who was Lillian's friend. Warner? No, Wheeler. That was it, and she spoke urgently to Kitty. The two moved into the living room, so George descended as far as he could while remaining hidden.

Miss Wheeler was crying and somewhat incoherent, but he quickly got the gist of her message. Lillian Holmes had attempted suicide last night, and had written a note to her best friend explaining her reasoning. So, the knife he'd dropped had done the trick. But Phillip would spot the scenario instantly. Nothing to do but run.

"I'm so sorry, Bess," Kitty exclaimed below. "She did seem upset when she was here, but I thought her perhaps a bit ill with the beginnings of a fever or some other physical ailment."

"Yes, it certainly took us all by surprise, except for Dr. Schneider, her physician. He's admitted her...*committed* her, to the hospital. For observation only, I pray. I hope it is a short stay, but he is greatly concerned. She is sedated and heavily guarded, lest she try to hurt herself again."

George had told many tall tales and listened to many in his day, so he knew absolutely that Miss Wheeler was not an accomplished liar, although she was doing her best.

"Heavily guarded?" Kitty repeated. "My, this is serious indeed!"

George groaned at her naiveté. So, this was a message from Lillian directly: Do not try to kill me again, for I am now surrounded and you will not reach me so easily.

"It is for the best." Bess's voice broke, and George realized the girl wasn't sure of her facts at all. Perhaps Lillian's spirit *was* broken.

"So, how can I help you?" Kitty asked. "Why have you come here?"

Bess took a deep breath. "As you say, she seemed rather upset last night. I wondered if you noticed what occurred during the séance that might have been...disturbing for her? I noticed nothing of obvious importance."

Oh, Kitty. Tread carefully here, lest you betray your beloved and his brother.

"Perhaps the séance itself, as communication beyond the veil, might be upsetting to someone as sensitive as she seems?" George could practically feel Kitty's discomfort, could practically hear the thoughts spinning in her head as she tried to find an acceptable reply. "You said the subject of her mother is difficult. I know Madam Pelosi meant no harm, as she told me she knew Lillian's mother—"

Damnation.

"Did you say the woman knows who Lil's mother is? Truly?"

"No. No, I meant that she communicated with her spirit. She made that rather clear."

"Oh," Bess replied, but doubt tinged her voice. She recognized that it was Kitty now who was that lousy prevaricator. So, she wasn't a complete fool.

"And begging your pardon, Kitty," the Wheeler girl went on, "but I must ask. There is nothing about the Orleans brothers or this household that would have contributed in any way to Lillian's state? She conversed a while with George. Perhaps something in *their* exchange?"

"Of course not!"

But the Wheeler girl looked around, and her mission became clear to George: find him, learn if he was still in Baltimore.

"How long have you known Phillip? It seems no one knows much about him."

"I assure you, Phillip had nothing to do with Miss Holmes's breakdown. He's barely exchanged a dozen words with her!"

"And George? Is he about? Perhaps he could assist me."

Kitty's silence turned George's legs to stone. Finally, his brother's beloved stood so quickly that her chair tumbled over. "I am sorry, Miss Wheeler, but I must end this interview. I have many items on my agenda today. Please tell Miss Holmes that I wish her a speedy recovery."

"I see," the blonde girl said, recognizing the lack of answer for the answer it was. "Yes, I will do so."

"Jameson will show you out."

George leapt up to the hallway and ducked into a closet as Kitty ran up the stairs, whispering curses to make a sailor blush. Bess accepted her coat and mumbled at Jameson as he helped her.

"What's that miss?"

"I said that the game is afoot."

"I'm sorry, miss, I do not understand."

"No matter. I do now."

Once Miss Wheeler was gone, George hurried down the stairs and called to Jameson.

"Sir?"

"Did you hear what transpired between the women?"

"I would never—"

"I've no time for games, Jameson!"

The butler nodded.

"Is it true? That Miss Holmes has been sent to a hospital?" George knew the best source of gossip in any household. The butlers and scullery spread word faster than a telegraph.

"Sir, yes. In the middle of the night. Quite tragic. A lovely, well-liked woman, so young—"

"Where did they take her? To Hopkins?"

"Why, no, sir. To the institution. Spring Grove Asylum, in the country. And not her first trip there, I heard."

"Blazes! What idiots."

So the first interesting mortal woman in a century had been swept away, by his actions, without him even having a chance to spend an hour in her extraordinary company. It wouldn't do. *How dare they take my Lillian!*

"What's the racket, Georgy?" Phillip looked cross as he descended the stairs.

"They've thrown Miss Holmes into the lunatic asylum, is the racket."

"Truly? Well, I'm surprised, but after all she did crawl around in the mud on Saturd—"

"She was looking for footprints, you idiot! You're as stupid and inattentive as these mortals!"

"What in God's name are you talking about?"

Tread a little more lightly, George. You may need Phillip yet.
"Oh, never mind. That will be all, Jameson."

When the butler was out of earshot, George grabbed his brother by the arm and pulled him close. "Look, I don't have time for the full novel, so I'll give you the captions. I'm certain Lillian is a morphine addict, and as you observed is a bit unusual in other ways for a woman of society. She is, however, not insane. She shot her pistol at a suspected intruder, got a bit bloody, and they thought she'd tried to commit suicide."

Phillip sank into a chair and covered his face. "Oh, George, how could you? You followed her home? Do you understand what this means?"

"Of course I do! Don't be so selfish! Well, don't be more selfish than me. Think of her, languishing in that awful place."

"How do you know she's languishing? How do you know the place is awful? Perhaps they are healing her and she truly requires the attention."

George squatted before Phillip and rested his hands on his knees to keep their eyes level. "Phillip, I know you've given up on me. Many times. I don't blame you at all; I've given up on myself. I was ready to leave Baltimore last night for good. I haven't broken my promise to you and Kitty, although I came close. But in my heart of hearts I know I wouldn't have finished the job. Lillian Holmes would still be alive, even if she hadn't had a damned pistol in bed with her. I can't explain why, but it's the truth."

Why? For a moment I remembered what it felt like to be human, to want a lover, to want a partner. It will make this life so much worse, that memory. Damn her. I will put it out of my mind soon.

"If doesn't matter, George. You've unleashed hell on my household! Threatened my life with Kitty! We'll have to leave Baltimore, and she loves it so. Damn you!"

"Hate me or love me, we must get Lillian out of that place."

"How? Would you turn yourself in?" His brother's eyes pleaded *no*, and George felt a bit of warmth and hope. Perhaps Phillip wasn't ready to be free of him quite yet.

"I don't think that would do the job. Not without revealing what I am. What *we* are."

"Does Lillian know about us? Does she know about her own mother?"

"Annaluisa loves to flap that loose tongue of hers, doesn't she? But, no. I don't think so. Well, I'm not sure." *Why did you feel the need to tell her what you are! Could she have remembered it in her state?*

"My God, what will I tell Kitty?"

"Tell her to ready a guest room."

"You are not serious?"

"At least she will see that I can help save a mortal instead of murder one, if indeed I am lucky enough to succeed. I caused this situation, and I have the rare inclination to fix it."

Phillip leaned back and sighed. "I don't know what is more shocking. That you say you give a damn about the woman, or that I believe you."

CHAPTER ELEVEN

An unwelcome getaway.

"I want to see her," Lillian mumbled, but the doctor either didn't hear or ignored her. Perhaps she hadn't actually spoken? Her eyes were shut, and everything was awhirl.

"My uncle will not tolerate this... You must speak with him... I will give you the address..."

What is his address? What is his name? Her head throbbed and her stomach turned as she opened her eyes to the dimly lit room. She saw only shadows at first but heard the low murmuring of a woman. She strained to hear the words then found them baffling: The stranger repeated a nursery rhyme in a precise cadence over and over.

The stench of soiled bedclothes made her stomach worse, and Lillian tried to sit only to find herself restrained with burlap straps. How long had she been asleep? And why did things look fuzzy? She tried to blink the blurriness away, but she still saw two of everything: Dr. Schneider at the foot of her bed times two, a stand with a pitcher on it doubled, a lamp that flickered side to side.

And there, off to the side, the most horrifying sight. The Jackal, watching, arms folded across his chest, a grin upon his twisted pocked face. Or was it a frown?

In horror she realized she couldn't feel her legs and tried to kick the blanket away. The blanket moved slightly and she understood she still had legs; they only felt dead. The Jackal moved toward the doctor and whispered something.

"What did you do to me? What did you give me?"

Someone behind her moaned and babbled incoherently, but she couldn't turn to see who stood there.

"Listen to me!" she shouted. But no one understood or cared. For she was the person babbling incoherently, she realized in horror. How had she lost the ability to speak? Would she be trapped in this Purgatory forever?

A prick at her arm made warmth flood through her vein and she faded into dreamless twilight.

CHAPTER TWELVE

Miss Holmes is rescued.

"I'd like to speak with Miss Wheeler, please!" George requested curtly.

There's little time, so little time. Angered by the details that made his life tiresome on a mundane day and impossible today, he barely had patience for the butler who requested George produce a card. He'd sprung out of his house the moment the sun set and literally flown the ten city blocks to the Wheeler house. He'd first considered venturing out in daylight, then weighed that he needed his full strength to rescue Lillian and decided that the rescue would be best under cover of night.

"It's rather late, sir, but I'll see if she's in."

The butler turned his back, and George held the door open and pressed past.

Bess stood in the foyer behind the servant, shock and horror etched across her face. She nonetheless found the nerve to take a deep breath and motion for the butler to leave. "Come in, Mr. Orleans. My father and mother are home, as are both my brothers."

"We don't have time for that, Miss Wheeler. I am not here to accost you, no matter what you might believe. You must listen carefully, as Lillian's freedom may hang in the balance."

Bess held her hand to her mouth. "That is exactly what she wrote in her letter to me. She told me to find you, but to—"

"To be careful? I imagine she told you not to come alone, but being nearly as pigheaded as she, you did anyway. Well, you found me. I'm here now."

"It's very confusing. On the one hand she said you threatened her, but it seems on the same night she wrote me to find you. I hear that she had a gash on her neck and fired her pistol several times. That was your doing, wasn't it?"

George grimaced. "Yes. I misinterpreted her feelings for me and pursued her. She mistook me for a robber, or for that terrible murderer loosed on Baltimore, and she fired at me. Fortunately she is not a good marksman. She tripped and hurt her neck on the andiron." Pausing, he chastised himself for not thinking the story through thoroughly. Did the woman even have a fireplace in her room?

"That was a terrible thing to do to her! I am glad she shot at you—and missed." Bess's face changed as the picture crystallized. "Oh! Then you can corroborate her story, and they will know she was not about killing herself. We must hurry to see the Adencourts. They must hear what you have to say and contact the doctor. That is why Lil wanted me to visit you."

"No!" Bess jumped at his tone, which George immediately softened. "No, Miss Wheeler. I cannot open myself up to that kind of scrutiny. More I cannot say about it, except to assure you that I have Lillian's interests at heart. In any case, it seems that the…Adencourts, did you say their name was? Yes, the Adencourts and the doctor rushed quickly to judge her actions and might not be so quick to have her released."

"That is likely the Jackal's doing."

"The Jackal?"

"A Mr. Pemberton, the solicitor in charge of Lil's fortune. They treat her as if she's a child instead of a brilliant, mature…well, perhaps she's unusual, but nevertheless—"

"Damnation. I take it Lillian dislikes Mr. Pemberton, given his moniker? Does she believe him to be after her wealth?"

Bess nodded. "She cares more about her freedom than money. But I've worried for her. I do not believe she attempted suicide, but her state of mind recently..." She bit her lip. "She's been obsessed. Would it hurt so much for her to stay there a bit longer? Doctor Schneider is a good friend and has taken care of her for many years. I cannot imagine he would allow anything to go wrong. Perhaps she does need watching over?"

"Did she not say in her letter that you were to do all in your power to free her? Do you understand some of the treatments your wonderful Doctor Schneider will likely give to a patient he considers mentally unstable? Have you not heard of the suffering of the insane in most of these so-called healing houses? They are little more than prisons at best, and some are veritable torture chambers. Surely you know that your friend has an opiate addiction. Half of what ails her is in those little pills and potions she consumes. The rest is part and parcel of a brilliant, spirited woman in an age of constraints and boredom. They can do nothing to heal that. She does not need more confinement!"

Bess wiped a tear and sat. "I tried to make her stop. Why didn't I do more? God help her."

George didn't care much about the young woman or her guilt, but she reminded him of Phillip: earnest, good-natured, a bit naïve. The type that bored him to distraction, and yet here was a valuable ally. "There is no way to stop an opiate addict from self-destruction by simply telling them what to do. It is not your fault; my suspicion is that it is not her fault."

"It is as if you truly do know her, Mr. Orleans. But I don't have power over...well, anyone. What weapon do I have to fight the Jackal or the doctor to make them release her?"

George held out both arms and bowed. "Voila, Miss Wheeler."

"What will you do?" She paced again, certainly wondering if she could trust him. "What am *I* to do? Are you certain it is best that she be freed?"

"I caused her great distress, and I aim to fix that with or without your help. I am going now to retrieve her and bring her to my home."

Miss Wheeler wrung her hands. "This feels like one of her Sherlock Holmes stories. I wish now I'd have read them. Perhaps I could be of more assistance."

George smiled. "Ah, she and I do have something in common then, for I am a reader of the same stories. I have a part for you to play, Watson."

"She calls me that at times. I fear I'm a very poor detective." The blonde girl shook her head. When she looked up, however, her eyes were full of determination. "But I will do whatever it takes."

"I believe you will; you are a formidable ally. I underestimated you, Miss Wheeler, and for that I owe you an apology."

"If you help my Lillian, then you owe me nothing and I will be in your debt forever."

One obstacle overcome.

Less than an hour later, George leapt across a stream trickling through the farmland and the country estates that fronted Asylum Lane. Spring Grove loomed on a hill, lights burning in many windows at an hour when most slept.

Twenty-four hours. He'd spoken to Lillian for the first time only a day ago, and now he felt an urgency to be with her again that belied their brief acquaintance. Half tempted to walk in the front door and bash anyone who got in his way, he took a cleansing breath. It wouldn't do to have half of the city searching for a kidnapper. She would have to seem escaped—or to have been released, perhaps with the assistance of one of the employees.

As he approached the massive building, he noted that all the windows were barred. How would he find her in that maze from the outside?

I'll work my way down.

A leap to the roof, four stories up, and he had a view of the twinkling lights of the harbor sloping to the north far in the distance. Baltimore. George took in the view for a moment. Phillip was there, and a few acquaintances. Beyond that, the city held nothing for him. But it would mean a great deal to Lillian, he guessed.

Never mind that, he thought. *You will leave and she will stay and all will be right with the world.*

The escape door on the roof opened with a solid pull and he was in, creeping lightly down an unlit staircase where he heard not a mortal peep. Still, this was unlikely the mortuary, which would be the lowest floor. But he felt no warmth as he ran his hands over the grey stone and continued down to the next level.

The scents of mortals wafted out through the landing, and he opened a large wooden door an inch to see who was about. A man in a drab uniform sat on a stool at the far end of the hallway, snoring. George hoped for the oaf's sake that he stayed asleep and crept to the first door.

Through the bars in an opening, he saw ten or more cots with men sleeping, one awake and staring at the door, eyes going wide when he saw George. George put his finger to his mouth and the man smiled sadly. No plea for help, no fear, but perhaps there was recognition that someone would be freed tonight.

Each of six rooms was the same, all men. George walked right past the guard to descend to the next floor which had many doors— and the vibration of females. *She is here.* He imagined he could almost hear her heartbeat.

In one room, a nurse reprimanded a patient who sounded very distressed. He prayed it wasn't Lillian. No, here she was, in a different chamber, her long hair pouring over her shoulder, sleeping or staring out the window, back toward him.

George freed the padlock with a single pull and gently opened the door. Would she cry out in terror to see the man who had nearly killed her the night before, or would she cry tears of relief to see her rescuer? Or, no doubt having been drugged, would she even notice his presence?

He weighed how to approach her when she turned suddenly and looked at him. She tried to speak, but her words were barely audible. At first she appeared terrified, and with good reason. She looked dreadful, her skin far too pale, her pulse slow in his ears.

George saw a tear roll down her cheek. He moved closer, putting a finger to his lips. He knelt near her, and he shook his head, her agony tearing at him. Yes, I want your blood, he thought. Yes, I want my safety, and you are a direct impediment to that. But I do not want to kill you. It would be like crushing the first flower of spring. She was not the scum of the Fell's Point docks, not an idiot of no consequence. No, Lillian Holmes, in another century, in a fantasy in which he wasn't a soulless killer, might have been the love of his life.

He wiped away her tear.

"Am I alive?"

It clearly pained her to speak, and he took her hand in his. "Alive, yes, and perhaps, before long, well."

With her eyes, she indicated her restraints. Flooded with relief at that bit of trust, George brushed her hair from her damp brow. Her eyes were rimmed in dark circles, and she had a bruise on her cheek. *I will kill whoever did that.* Of course, he reminded himself, the bandage on her neck was his doing.

She seemed to be having difficulty focusing on his face. "I want…"

"No, don't fall asleep! Tell me what you want!" He pulled the straps from her wrists and ankles. As tenderly as he could, he lifted her torso to lean against his body, and she released a sigh that broke his heart.

"I want to see her," she mumbled, with such determination to get the words out that he thought she might faint from exertion.

"You will find your mother. You will see her."

"No… I want to see her. The baby."

George pulled back and stared into her eyes as he steadied her. *Baby?*

"Water…"

He felt her head and groaned. She needed much more than water.

"The city wants me…it wants me to ride into the harbor. It wants to kill me."

George grimaced. "What the blazes did they give you? No more talking now. I will protect you from the city." *And may the city protect you from me.*

He found a glass and filled it from her washing pitcher, the only water in the room. Swirling a bit in his mouth to ensure it wasn't fouled, he then held the glass up to her parched lips. "Slowly. Only a little to start."

She sipped while he wiped her face of perspiration and dirt with a cloth, and then he wrapped her in a blanket.

"We must go now, Lillian. You are safe." It took a moment for him to tear the bars from the window before he realized it was too narrow for him to get through alone, much less holding Lillian. "Back the way I came, then."

He scooped her into his arms, pressed her head against his shoulder, trying to ignore the scent of blood still on her neck that made his entire being thirst for her. When did they last change that bandage? God, the world over, these places were hell.

Quickly he moved out into the hall and up the stairs. The guard was still asleep, and he met no resistance. For that George was thankful, though he equally wanted to make someone pay. When he pushed open the flap door to the roof, a rush of fresh air blew Lillian's hair in a swirl across his face, and he pressed a kiss on her forehead.

"Mr. Orleans," she whispered, and he nearly dropped her in surprise. "Will you kill me again tonight?"

"No, I don't think so. Will you shoot at me tonight?"

"Perhaps. But I've misplaced my pistol."

George smiled, but it was a pained expression. She might shoot him again, but she'd have to survive this fever first.

CHAPTER THIRTEEN

Perchance to dream.

Lillian floated down a river on her back, watching trees and filmy clouds of myriad colors flicker by. Terror came from the knowledge that she approached a waterfall and would die when the river carried her down that endless drop. She tried to fight her way to the shore but her limbs wouldn't move, tried to cry out but she couldn't make a sound.

She started awake and clutched at the bed. The room spun at first, but she finally was able to focus on the source of the voices that blurred in the background. Three figures, two men and a woman.

The last several days rushed back in an instant, and she realized she'd been freed from the institution but wasn't free of her catastrophic situation. She quickly shut her eyes to avoid alerting her...captors? Saviors? Who were Kitty and the Orleans brothers? *What* were they?

Lillian tried to hold on to silence as she spied, but the aches and anxiousness in her body made it difficult. Her legs moved restlessly without her permission, and she couldn't stop fretting with the blanket. *My heart has never raced this fast. Is it terror, or am I dying?*

"Why did you bring the Wheeler woman into it?" Phillip asked, frantic and angry.

"She can be trusted, as long as she believes our goals match hers," George replied.

"Poor thing looks terrible," Kitty murmured, thankfully not looking over at Lillian. "Can I do nothing to help her?"

"She'll look terrible for a while but should recover. I'm certain the brilliant doctor gave her more of some opiate, thinking she had a breakdown."

"Didn't she? Wouldn't you?" Kitty's voice didn't hide an apparent loathing for George. "A man steals into your room and takes a nice chunk out of your neck, then isn't hurt when you put two bullets into him. How could she possibly be sane after that!"

"It simply wasn't like that. In any case, I could have killed her and I did not. Despite your emotionally driven lack of reasoning, that should be the proof you both need of my rehabilitation. I am not a murderer."

"Don't get snide with Kitty!"

"Look, the point is that we must make her well, and as I've gone through some similar rehabilitations, although eons ago, I am the person to nurse her to health. It will take a few days for her to be past the worst. Then I'll leave Baltimore. I believe that once she is clearheaded, you will find that she has far more than adequate intelligence and resources to care for herself. She can end the charade by actually joining her friend Bess at the Wheeler country estate, and they can return to the city together, her recuperation complete. Voila!"

"To hell with you and your voila!" Kitty stormed from the room.

"It will be all right, Phillip. This will be the last penance you'll endure for the sin of being born my brother. I'll be so far away, for so long, you'll barely remember me."

"What of Marie de Bourbon? I thought you insisted upon my help, upon building a following with which to battle her?"

"My choices are to kill Lillian Holmes so that she does not betray me and stay, or to find a part of the world in which she,

Marie, and anyone else who loathes me cannot find me. I do not intend to kill Miss Holmes."

"So dramatic, George. Let me know if you need anything. I must go soothe an angry Irishwoman. Haven't quite got the knack of that yet."

Lillian suppressed a relieved sigh, for as far as she could tell George's intentions seemed good, unless he was lying to his own brother. Was he capable of that? Surely, and much more. But why had he rescued her, then? She did have some hope that she'd awake permanently from this most inconvenient nightmare.

If only I'd gone to sleep when I should have; if only I'd never looked out my window to see the Leaping Man. But here he was, taking a seat next to the bed, wiping the perspiration from her forehead and humming a tune she didn't recognize. No, she'd gotten something wrong. The man simply was not a murderer. He would have an explanation about her neighbor, about why he'd been about that night. But who was this Marie whom he was fixing to battle?

She allowed herself a bit more time to clear her head and think how to approach this most odd of men. *Vampire, indeed.* He was no more a vampire than Madam Pelosi could speak with the dead. Still, he had somehow wounded her neck and she had to understand why her bullets bloodied him without seeming to slow him down. Perhaps he wore a suit of armor under that coat?

A sudden violent chill took her body and stopped her train of thought. *God, how long will this go on? Is this what the doctor warned me of?*

"Shhhh," George whispered. He sat on the side of the bed and then gingerly leaned down beside her.

Too exhausted to fight her symptoms in secret any longer, she opened her eyes. He didn't seem surprised at all, and he smiled.

"How long have you been listening?"

"Long enough, I think. You take great liberties lying next to me."

He smiled again. "You take great liberties by occupying my bed. You must explain yourself."

"I, explain? I don't understand any of this, but I will, and soon. In the meantime, I thank you for what you have done."

"It is my pleasure, and small payment for my error in your room. Now, sleep some more. You will need your strength."

"For what?"

"Tomorrow will be terrible. After that, it will be somewhat less terrible. Then you will have a choice to make."

"I think you made it for me. You took me from the asylum."

"No, this is a choice you must make."

"I choose to become the first great female detective in America. Mr. Arthur Conan Doyle himself said that nothing need stop me." Why did she feel free to say such a thing to this near stranger? It must be a symptom.

His smile caressed her weary body and spirit. "I do believe you. And once free of this poison, I don't believe anything can stop you, not even the evil Moriarty himself. Sleep now. I will keep vigil."

"The wolf guards the henhouse."

"We are more equal than you might believe. I wasn't so unlike you a long time ago."

"What do you mean?"

"Just sleep, Lil. No need to think tonight."

She felt a sudden jolt. "Addie and Thomas will be so frightened to learn I'm gone."

"They think you in the country recuperating with Bess, who convinced them that the doctor thought it would be a welcome change of scenery. I've arranged it. We'll speak of that soon, though. Sleep! Turn that blasted brain off for the night!"

He put his arm around her waist to warm her, and it worked; through every fiber of muscle, every inch of bone heat poured. Lillian rested her head against his shoulder and tried to stay awake as long as possible to feel what it was to be in his arms.

He would leave when she was well, he'd said. That was for the best, she thought as he pressed another kiss to her head.

CHAPTER FOURTEEN

Hidden treasures.

"Another visitor! Oh, blazes, why did Kitty bring the Langhan sisters here?"

Phillip cursed and drew the curtain. "Are you sure Lillian will be quiet?"

George nodded. "Unless she begins retching and they hear it."

Kitty winced in apology as she ushered Etta and Agnes into the living room.

"How lovely to see you both again so soon," George murmured. His tone was lost on Etta, but the sharper of the sisters, Agnes, raised a brow.

"We were so upset to hear about Lillian Holmes." Etta seemed sincerely concerned.

"I told you she will be fine, Etta," Kitty said. "The doctor released her into the care of her friend, Elisabeth Wheeler, as she has no family herself. I trust she's having a lovely time at the country house, feeling better already."

"We did not call on the Holmes residence as we hardly know Lillian, so we stopped at the Wheeler residence. No one was about!"

George willed himself to silence, as Kitty was handling things well enough. But the busybodies had to go!

He noticed Agnes examining him and turned toward her. *Hell, she's a physician, George. She'll smell a rat. Hit it face on, then.*

"Dr. Langhan, it is a pity Lillian was not taken to the new hospital—Johns Hopkins, is it? You could have cared for her then."

"Dr. Schneider is…adequate. I do not make asylum visits, but I suppose he takes that duty on out of necessity."

"Ah, I see. Perhaps you could grant a second opinion when she returns from the country." *Competitive bitch. What a stroke of luck. She doesn't like him at all.*

"I would not interfere with Dr. Schneider's treatment of his patient, although I do think a female physician can understand some of what might be troublesome to a female patient. In my opinion, those in my profession are quick to judge women as frail and nervous when in fact they may simply be going through a normal life stage or some sadness associated with a failed marriage or lost pregnancy. You see—"

"Agnes! This is not a lecture hall," Etta chided and pulled at her sister's arm. "We must go if we are to make the art auction, which is why we came." She turned to Kitty. "More of Theodore Robinson's paintings. You should come with us. All the right people will be there."

"Oh, yes! Let's hurry." Kitty ushered the women to the door with a backward glance over her shoulder that sent daggers through George.

Phillip sat down and ran his hand through his hair. "Who is next? The new mayor? Why have they all descended upon us?"

"Yes, it's getting tricky. Hopefully they've all believed the tale. If the Wheelers decide to join their daughter at their own country home we'll have a problem. But I think I persuaded them that Lillian needed solitude. Have we thought of everyone?"

"I've not met Dr. Schneider, but it seems to me he'll become aware rather quickly that his patient escaped from a supposedly secure institution. What are you going to do about that, Georgy?"

"I could kill him, I suppose. That seems a bit rash. I put off that troublesome detail a bit too long, didn't I? And there's evidently some greedy solicitor unlikely to overlook the parts of my story that do not make sense."

"Parts? The entire thing. You should have just left."

"You've seen her state. She wouldn't have survived the week in that place."

"So, you'll kill indiscriminately for centuries, but somehow you'll turn your life upside down to save this one woman? She is not your type, and if she were you would have turned her already. What are you up to, George?"

He had no idea.

"What is the worst the solicitor and the doctor can do?" George mused. "Go to visit Lillian, hear some new tale from Bess, go on a chase that will send him in circles? How far is it to Sandy Point?"

Phillip shrugged. "Several hours or so by carriage? I'm not sure. I think you have a day or two at most before he makes some report to the police."

"Two days…" Only two days to help her get well and get her back to Bess's care? "Time always seemed the one commodity we had."

"Their lives are measured in days and minutes. You are reminded of that now. I feel it whenever I'm with Kitty."

"That is different. She is your fiancée. And you have the option of extending her short life. I envy you, Phillip."

"What do you envy, George? Is there more to this than undoing an injustice? You've known her two days."

"Don't be stupid. In another three days I'll be on my way and I won't even think about her."

"Who's stupid, brother?"

"Ah, there is the retching I warned her about. The end of this phase of her nightmare is near."

"Two days. Take her to the seaside, and for God's sake do not bite her again. Or we'll start this whole mess over."

"Wouldn't think of it."

But he had thought of it, nearly nonstop. He blamed his brother for leading him down this dull, dull path of righteousness. Phillip always was soft where George was sharp, forgiving and amiable considering all he'd endured. Never mind, George thought. Once Lillian joined her friend, he could leave his brother's benign habits behind and go wherever the wind and the smell of blood took him, take Marie de Bourbon on a useless merry chase.

Resolved to move the inevitable parting forward, he took the stairs two at a time to check on Lillian. She'd washed her face in the basin and sat on the edge of the bed, dabbing her cheeks with a cloth.

"You look dreadful, Miss Holmes."

"I've you to thank for that, I suppose, Mr. Orleans."

"You have your morphine and laudanum habit to thank. The worst should be over now, at least physically. I take it you have a severe craving for a dram of some elixir? That will hopefully lessen as well."

"How long?" Her hands shook as she folded the washcloth. "I want to crawl from my body."

"You want to scream and cry and pound the walls. But you are free—it has left your body." He paused. "When did you start? The longer you have been addicted, the worse the sentence."

Lillian shook her head and straightened her dressing gown, borrowed from Kitty. It hung loosely, and she looked like a frail china doll.

"It is truly none of my business; you are correct." *But tell me anyway. I want to know it all, and I don't know why.*

Lillian nodded. "I will wash, and if Miss Twamley would be so kind as to loan me a dress and shoes I'll be on my way. You have been a great help."

"Oh, Lil, so formal. Haven't we shared a bed at least twice? Or thrice, if you count the asylum."

"A few minutes in a sickbed does not an assignation make, Mr. Orleans. I want to leave."

"You aren't ready. You must rest and eat. You'll need money, which I can provide, and your own clothes."

"How will I get… Aileen. We must ask my maid Aileen to help. She is a loyal friend."

George nodded. "What is the best way to contact her?"

"Your man to one of the Musketeers, her little brothers who now reside in my home."

How had she fallen into such an addiction? Lillian's home sounded bright, her days so full of life. "So many who care for you. You have no doubt recruited them into your…investigations?" It only made sense. She was clearly fashioning her own Baker Street Irregulars.

Lillian sat up straight and stared into his eyes. It stirred both the best and worst in him. His veins sang with the promise of a meal; his groin throbbed with the promise of satisfaction. But his heart also ached at what he could never have. More. Of what, he couldn't say, for it was something he hadn't had in his long life. But more, more of her.

"You mock me. It does not matter."

But her expression said it mattered a great deal, another blow to an already beaten down heart and soul. He moved quickly to fix the erroneous assumption. "Not at all. If my goal were to become a great sleuth, I would also recruit those who seemed…invisible."

He smiled at the memory of the motley crew descending upon her. "I saw you once, from a hotel window. The details don't matter, but you seemed happy to see those boys. At least, I assume it was them. They were accompanied by a rather large hound."

"Mr. Abraham Lincoln…" She trailed off, a note of fear in her voice. "You watched me from a window? Why?"

Damnation. "A complete coincidence, I assure you. I saw a lovely woman, a true beauty. A stranger who no doubt lived a rather ordinary life with a wealthy husband." He shrugged. "I was wrong. You are lovely, but you are not ordinary."

"Nor are you ordinary, Mr. Orleans." She combed her fingers through her long hair, and the movements of her delicate hands and her words tugged at him. "Did I not also see you from a window? Did you not climb through one only a few nights ago?"

"Lillian, concentrate on your health. You needn't worry about your safety. I came to Spring Grove to help you. Surely you know that if I meant you harm I have had ample opportunity to wreak havoc."

"Yes, at least that is what I keep telling myself. But…you *are* the Leaping Man."

The Leaping Man? Ah, he understood. He wasn't ready, though, not for either the truth or a lie. "I visited one of your neighbors. Unfortunately, that same night, her brother met his untimely end at his own hand. I can only plead guilty to the assignation, not the death."

Leave it be, my dear.

"There might or might not have been an assignation, but there was undoubtedly a murder. I know of no other man who can leap from two stories without killing himself—or does your brother possess equal talents?"

"No," George whispered. "Phillip would not hurt a flea if he could avoid it." *Certainly leave him be, Lillian. I have ruined too much for him.*

"I believe that. And two nights ago? Why did you come if not to cause me harm? What are these marks upon my neck? They were not made by a knife."

"You do not remember our kiss? I am sorry, Lil, as I thought we were of like mind. A little nibble upon the neck is part of my romantic repertoire; no doubt you found that distasteful. Phillip tells me I'm quite egotistical about my power over women. I did not expect to be shot, however."

"You seem none the worse for wear. Explain that away, Mr. Orleans."

"You are as poor a shot as I am a reader of a lady's interest in me. A few nicks, a bit of blood, and now I am fine. Dear Miss Holmes, I am trying to right the horror I put you through. I am leaving this fine city as soon as that is accomplished."

She nodded and scooped her limp hair into a bundle. "I have solved a crime perpetrated by you, and thus you are fleeing before I can turn you in to the authorities?"

He did not answer that. "I am leaving for good. I am off to explore other parts of the world, and to leave my brother and his soon-to-be bride in peace. You have witnessed the effect I have on them."

Lillian fussed with her hair a bit more. "What of the late mayor? Would you also claim to have had an assignation with one of his household—or maybe with him? It seems you are a dangerous lover."

He sniffed out a chuckle and choked back unwelcome grief. "So, that is what you think of me? I will not try to dissuade you from that opinion. It does not matter. More I cannot say. Surely my word means nothing to you, but I give it nonetheless. I will not harm you, and I will leave this city, not to return in your lifetime."

"And when will you leave?" she whispered to the view out the window.

He sighed and ignored the sadness in her voice, lest he grab onto it and create a new fantasy of being with her.

"Are you well enough to eat a biscuit and take a few sips of tea? I believe it's time for us to try to fatten you up. I will get a message to Aileen to bring some of your things, and then I will take you to Sandy Point myself."

"Thank you." She wouldn't look at him now. Not at all.

"Perhaps a warm bath would be welcome. I will have one prepared and then send up some food. Goodnight, Miss Holmes."

"Goodnight, Mr. Orleans. Oh, may I ask one more thing?"

Here it comes. Careful, George.

"Was I imagining that you claimed to be a vampire? I am certain I heard you say that."

"A vampire?" George laughed. "Oh my, you've had a difficult few days. Wait until I tell Phillip that one!"

He left the room quickly. But as George shut the door behind him, he felt as if he shut it on the first glimmer of life he'd felt for eons.

Best to throw away that key, Georgy boy.

CHAPTER FIFTEEN

Into the country.

Lillian glanced out the window of the carriage, having trouble distinguishing their location in the darkness.

George Orleans was a poor traveling companion. He'd spoken precious few words in the hours since they left his home. He'd explained they would travel at night to avoid anyone seeing her, but she thought he was the one on the lam, as Mr. Pinkerton would likely say.

She'd failed miserably. The Leaping Man was to be her first case, and although Providence had threaded him deeply into her life, she'd yet to get to the heart of the matter—although she felt fairly certain he had a hand in two murders. Also, he hadn't become a proper nemesis. He'd caused her enough trouble; that much was true. But he'd also done what she couldn't do for herself, what Dr. Schneider hadn't been able to do. She had no morphine or laudanum in her blood. The shaking had subsided, her appetite had returned, and she only thought of reaching for a pill or bottle every half-hour or so. George had assured her those fits of longing would eventually subside, as long as she kept her focus on the future.

In a way, she owed him so much. And now he would leave.

"Eight years," she whispered.

"Pardon?"

"You asked me how long. I started taking the pills for my nerves when I was sixteen."

He turned to face her, but she could barely make out his features in the darkness, as he'd not allowed any illumination inside the carriage. She'd supposed he wanted to sleep.

"It's not my concern."

Her heart dropped at his tone. Now she was a nuisance, so anxious was he to be on his way to see the mysteries of the world. Just another woman in a second-story room.

She jumped when he spoke again, much more loudly. "Sixteen? Oh, I am so very sorry."

"I will be fine."

In the darkness, he reached for her hand, found it and squeezed firmly. That cold grasp warmed her tired body. "No, Lillian, that is not what I mean. In Spring Grove, I thought you were hallucinating. You did speak of the city wanting to kill you."

"Yes, I might have said. In my worst nervous moments, I have succumbed to some odd notions. Would you like to hear the most remarkable?"

"More remarkable than Baltimore trying to kill you?"

"In the last few years, I took to reading novels to ease my nerves. At times I allowed myself to slip into various fantasies. The strongest of these is that I am actually a fictional character myself."

"Indeed?"

"The niece...the niece of Sherlock Holmes. I suppose because of my name. I know how this must sound to you."

"It sounds like a lovely fantasy, Lil. Who wouldn't want to have such an exciting family when you have none at all?"

And in one sentence, he'd said what she never spoke aloud. The Truth of Lillian Holmes. They were all gone. She fretted with her bag, wishing that there were a bottle of solace left there.

He kept her hand and squeezed again. "That is why I am a bit morose tonight. I am leaving the only family member who does not hate me, or at least doesn't hate me much. But Phillip is better off alone. I'm a bit wild for his liking."

"Yes, you are a bit wild, murdering and jumping out of windows and rescuing women from madhouses. I sense there is more to it than that, George? In fact, you told me more in a weak moment."

"Hmn. Nothing several hundred kilometers won't cure. But you are being a lady detective at the moment, and you will not catch me off guard, Miss Holmes."

She sniffed out a laugh.

He slid closer to her, and her heart sped at the contact. She briefly wondered if he'd kiss her again before they parted. Had she imagined how wonderful his lips felt, his hand along her hip? How could she crave a monster's touch?

"I have great sympathy for you, Lil. I have suffered a great deal in my life. My mother betrayed me in the most despicable fashion. My father abandoned my brother and me when we needed him most. I have craved something impossible since then. In many ways, we are similar. But your loss is the worst. Not only your mother, but a child."

Her blood ran to ice. "What?"

"Why, that is why you were given drugs at sixteen. No doubt you were hospitalized and then closeted at home, away from the judging eyes of society. You had a baby."

"Do not be ridiculous." *Who would have told him that? Bess never would have betrayed my secret.*

"And you never saw her."

"Who said that?"

"You did. In Spring Grove. I didn't understand it then, but I do now. I am so sorry. Did the father also leave you alone?"

She pulled her hand from his and clutched at her stomach to stop the churning. "I cannot speak about that."

"Of course you can. Don't you see? Those pills, those potions? Have they filled the void in your life? They never worked for me."

Lillian choked back a sob. "I am fine."

"Oh, my dear. Your life is so short. Why waste it pretending?" He pulled her into a hug, rubbed at her back, and the world fell out from under her feet. She collapsed in his embrace and sobbed for what seemed like an eternity.

"I am so sorry," she said at last. "I never cry."

"That is your problem, then. No wonder you are anxious. When I am gone you must speak with your friend Elisabeth on these matters, and perhaps to that dreadful Dr. Langhan who seems to favor female issues."

"It was a terrible mistake, and very long ago. I have paid the price. It is time to move on."

"My guess is that you fell in love. You were young. Someone else made the terrible mistake in not adhering to your wish to keep your child."

"They meant well."

I was never in love. There was no handsome boy. Her mood flattened, as it did whenever she dared to remember that horrible night so many years ago. Her limbs grew light, and she wondered why she'd felt anything at all towards George Orleans. Addie and Thomas were not to blame, were they? Why then did she want to scream at them? She wanted to scream at everyone, especially since being free of her medicine. What would take this awful pain away now? Perhaps if would have been best had George had killed her.

"Ah, are we at the Wheeler estate?"

So soon? Now the Leaping Man would leave?

"Estate may be an exaggeration," he went on. "It seems to be one of these cottages by the sea."

"Yes, they have had difficulties and were forced to put this cottage up for sale. Fortunately, it is still vacant."

She said no more, aching. He pulled her forward and hovered so close. His cool breath brushed across her cheek, and the pain of losing him broke through her emotional stupor. He'd opened up so many wounds, and now they would remain open. In desperation Lillian pulled him down into a kiss and lost herself in the taste of him, in the feel of his hands roaming her torso, in his body pressing against her.

He broke the kiss for a second and brushed the back of his hand against her cheek. "This is cruel. I want you badly."

And I, you. But how can I want a murderer, one who may not be human? How can I resist? He would think me a common whore. "Perhaps you can stay a while? I could make up a story for Bess…"

But she'd heard it in his voice. He would go from her life as mysteriously as he'd come.

The carriage stopped, and she heard the driver get down and pull her small sack from the compartment behind them. "I do not think I would turn you in," she announced. "I would be a friend rather than an enemy…"

"I have other enemies, and you would come to despise me in any case. Goodbye, Lillian Holmes."

"Goodbye, George Orleans."

The door opened, and she stepped from the carriage with the help of the driver. She didn't look back but walked up the path to see Bess waiting in the doorway, holding a lamp against the darkness. Only when the whip cracked and the wheels turned did she finally spin around, but the carriage was soon rounding the narrow bend of the sandy lane and George was gone forever from her life.

CHAPTER SIXTEEN

More difficult times.

Bess put the hairbrush down and rested her hands on Lillian's shoulders. "You look lovely again, although thin. I'll make tea and buttered bread and you will eat every crumb."

"Yes, mother." Lillian smiled at her friend's worried image in the vanity mirror and took a deep breath. It was her second morning at the cottage. The night had been more restful than the first, more restful than she'd thought possible. Despite the turmoil of the last weeks, the sounds of crickets and tree frogs and a gentle seaside breeze rustling through the loblolly pines outside her window had lulled her into dreamless sleep. Indeed, she wouldn't have to lie about recuperating at the Wheeler vacation home; recuperating she was, thanks to the Leaping Man. Of course, he had caused a good deal of her troubles.

"You're thinking about him again," Bess warned.

"Nonsense."

"You knew who I meant."

"Well, of course I did. Bess, I assure you that I am intrigued by the mystery and immune to every other aspect of the man. Or vampire. Or murderer. In any case, I shall likely not meet him again." While she kept the disappointment out of her voice, it crept into her chest and squeezed. His quick goodbye had felt so dismissive. Yes, well, that was all to be expected and certainly for the best.

Her friend sat next to her and stared at her in the mirror. "I know that Orleans enclave has turned our lives upside down. Lil, I have to tell you something. Are you truly feeling well?"

"I'm fine." *My hands shake constantly and my veins crave calming, but George assured me this will pass.* "Tell me what is on your mind. You are bored and wish to go out?"

Bess folded her arms and wiggled her foot. "Just because I don't carry a pistol and crawl around in mud looking for evidence, I am not stupid!"

"You most certainly are not. I have told you that you could be an admirable assistant... I'm sorry. Oh, Bess, you're my one true friend. I don't know why I talk that way. I imagine I try to imitate my uncle." She stopped herself. "My *pretend* uncle. I hardly know what I'm doing anymore. Tell me what's on your mind. Are you well? Is the family bearing up under their difficulties?" *I am too self-absorbed. I must find a way to be a better friend to her.*

"I am a good assistant," Bess agreed. "But I've lied to my entire family, gone calling on some of the strangest people I've ever encountered, perhaps even put myself in danger."

"Please forgive my foolishness."

"Although I am supposedly an idiot, I believe I have important information for you." Bess winced and squeezed Lillian's hand, and without another word Lillian knew the topic. The Truth of Lillian Holmes had surfaced more than once recently. It seemed to be in the air.

"It's about my heritage," she guessed. "I hope you have not been listening to that quack again."

Bess's cheeks colored. "Kitty slipped when I visited her. She mentioned your mother. I don't know how, but I am convinced that the quack has some true knowledge about her. Do you remember how eager she was to speak to you about it?"

Lillian swallowed the lump in her throat and nodded. She'd felt that George hid something about her family as well, although he hadn't discussed it openly. All her secrets boiled beneath a thin surface that was once a thick wall. What had become of the carefully built fortress that guarded her from pain and worry?

Bess touched her hand. "Lil, are you *certain* that your mother is dead? Have you pressed Addie and Thomas on the topic? Or asked the Jackal? Oh, look at your face. I am sorry I brought it up. I thought if there was a chance to know more—"

The tears came unbidden and unwelcome, burning her throat and chest. "I am no longer certain of anything. Does it matter? The woman wanted nothing to do with me."

Bess frowned and held Lillian's gaze. "How do you know that you were not snatched from her arms as your child was snatched from yours? Perhaps she has been looking for you for many years. Perhaps she is afraid you would not want to see her."

"I suppose I am paying doubly for my own mistake."

"For the love of God, stop punishing yourself for falling in love! The boy did not stay. That is his failure, not yours! You would have wed him, I know it. Don't you see, Lil? I know how empty…how lonely…"

There was no boy to wed. He did not flee. God help me.

"Go on. You are right. I fill my days with fantasies and pretend that I do not care about the rest. What would you have me do, Bess? Spend the rest of my life looking for an eight-year-old child who could live anywhere, who could be dead? Where would I begin? How would I begin to find the mother who left me?"

"Begin with the Orleans brothers, Kitty, and Madam Pelosi. They know something, and I believe they will be willing to help. Of course, you'll have to make sure they don't try to murder you again, if that is indeed what occurred."

"No, I don't think George tried to murder me. And he certainly rescued me from Spring Grove. But he is probably on a train or ship by now."

"Oh, such longing in your voice, Lil. You certainly need my help in picking out men more than you need my help with hats. Of course, he was most delicious to look at. I think I shall miss him, too, dark and menacing as he seemed. But we will call on Phillip and Kitty when we return home. And perhaps this time we should ask Officer Johnnie Moran to accompany us."

"No. We do not need Johnnie. I will get my pistol back from Thomas. We will learn what there is to know about my mother." And perhaps they would learn more about the Leaping Man as well.

"I do not think I'm cut out to be your Watson," Bess said with a sigh.

"My *Watson*? Why, whatever made you say that? You instructed me not to call you that!"

"George Orleans used it. If he weren't the devil, I'd say you were cut from the same cloth."

"Hardly."

But Lillian wondered. Where was he, the man who seemed to understand her more than she understood herself? Far away, no doubt. If he'd asked, would she have gone with him?

Why wonder? He is gone.

***

Lillian made a subtle motion to Bess to stay with her as Addie, Thomas, Aileen, and the three boys circled round her, Mr. Abraham Lincoln left to bark on the porch. She'd been gone only a few days, but the past now seemed like a different lifetime.

After tearful hugs and inquiries as to her health, she finally sat alone with Bess and Addie. The mantel clock seemed like a church gong, the parlor had become so quiet. Bess wanted to leave, Lillian knew it, but she needed her friend and now the two had no secrets. Well, one, but Lillian would take the identity of the father of her child to the grave.

"Dr. Schneider came by this morning, desperately concerned for you, Lil," Addie said. Her tone of disapproval, usually amusing, made Lillian bristle.

"I will speak with him in due course. Please do not concern yourself with that. If he asks again, please tell him to speak with me directly and that I will see him when I have time."

Addie sat up straight, a flicker of hurt on her face. Lillian pushed down the guilt that threatened to thwart her mission. *She* hadn't been the secret-keeper. *She* hadn't rewritten the past with silence. She'd just been a girl, a lonely, frightened girl.

"I love you, Addie, and I know you love me. But the time has come for us to speak frankly. I am no longer a child to be protected. No pain could be worse than this void I've carried for so long. Tell me the truth about my mother."

The color left Addie's face and she cast a quick glance at the doorway where Thomas lurked in shadow. "What do you mean, Lil? Why now?"

"Because I am ready to hear." *Am I? Where is my Leaping Man to give me courage? How dare he open this wound and then leave me alone to close it!*

"But we know nothing, Lil. Please, you will suffer another breakdown if you persist in this vein. I must send for Mr. Pemberton."

"That threat will no longer work on me." But Lillian shuddered and rubbed at her arms. The Jackal would never hurt her again; she would hire another solicitor and learn if she could free herself from him forever.

Thomas stood forward. "She's not a child, Addie. She has made the choice. We knew the day would come. It is her right."

"What do you know of such choices, Thomas?" the governess snapped.

"I know you blame me for our brothers' death, but they chose to follow me to war. I cannot change that. You cannot change Lillian's past. But it is *her* past, not yours. Secrets help no one."

Thomas limped to Lillian and pulled her by both hands to stand. "Addie and I have loved you from the start. We were in the employ of the elder Mr. Pemberton, me just back from the conflict and Addie in a state over my brothers. Mr. Pemberton told us of a sad case of an orphaned girl who would never need for anything save a family. Because we are brother and sister, we could not raise you as our child, of course. Instead, we did our best. We were never told the name of your mother or father…"

His long hesitation made Lillian's racing heart skip a beat. "Yes, go on, Thomas."

"But I had suspicions. At the time we heard of a young woman of society who disappeared mysteriously. I cannot remember her name. That is all I can tell you. I am sorry it isn't enough."

"What about the solicitor?" Bess asked. "Could he tell us about his client?"

"The elder Pemberton has been dead for years. The case went to his son, Francis. I doubt anyone knows the truth now."

"And was it the elder or the younger Pemberton who arranged for my baby to be taken from me? It was not you and Addie, I believe."

Thomas wrapped his arm around her shoulder, but the gesture didn't warm her. She felt cold and numb.

"No," Addie whispered. "We gave your baby to the Hebrew Orphan Asylum, along with a generous donation, at the advice of Mr. Francis Pemberton."

"How proper of you to give a donation as well. I assume the orphanage would have no knowledge of the name of the mother? No, of course not. Most improper."

"She's no doubt with a good family now, Lil," Bess said. Then she shook her head. "Blazes, I do not know that. I won't contribute to these awful secrets or try to soften them with platitudes."

"Thank you, Elisabeth. You have proven yourself to be the truest of friends. Let us get you home. That will be all, Addie and Thomas."

For the first time in her life, Lillian dismissed her guardians from the room. Addie rose, weeping, and left with Thomas holding her.

"It is not their fault, of course. But today I am angry. Tomorrow I shall make amends."

Bess rested her head on Lillian's shoulder. "I think I would be angry, too. And I understand why you drank those awful potions and ate those pills and…"

"And?"

"And why you pretended you were related to a man in a book."

Lillian sat and let out a curse. "I did what I needed to do. Now I can do what I choose to do."

"You will look for them, won't you?"

"Yes, I will. I do not know how, but I will. And I believe all my longing to become a great detective will finally serve me well."

"Then I will be your Miss Watson and help. To be truthful, a life spent longing after silly men and pretty dresses is leaving me a bit weary. If I am to live as an ugly crippled old maid, so be it. Perhaps it is time for me to learn how to shoot a pistol."

"Nonsense."

"I am glad to hear you say it."

"You will learn how to wield a small blade."

"Are you quite serious? Oh, my, why do I ask?"

***

"Damn it all!" George stared at the tunnel to the ferry to New York, knowing it was the last run of the evening, knowing what he should do, what he must do.

Get on it, he repeated to himself a dozen times until the Jersey City train conductor blew his whistle and yelled "Final call!" for the train going back south. To Manhattan, then to points west? Or back on the train to Baltimore? One more time, the conductor yelled "Final call!" and George nearly screamed in frustration.

At the last second he leapt from the platform onto the slowly moving train, and the conductor reached out to secure his landing, although he didn't need the help.

"Where to, sir?" he asked, withdrawing his ticket booklet.

"Straight into hell, no doubt." George shoved five dollars at the man to be left alone and took a seat in back corner of the filthy sooty car, wondering if he had finally gone insane. Marie de Bourbon, Madam Lucifer, wanted to kill him and might be as close as New Orleans. He'd sworn to leave Phillip and Kitty in peace, and what did he do instead? Take a train right back to the first place Marie would look for him. All for a mortal woman.

He laughed as the train emerged from the Hudson tunnel, revealing dilapidated buildings and abandoned machinery left to crumble by the side of the tracks. No doubt only he could make out the carcasses of modern society in the inky dark. A carcass, that was what he'd become, too. A hollow shell, neither living nor dead, worth nothing to anyone, except perhaps the price Madam Lucifer had put on his head. Wouldn't she be doing the world a service? One less monster draining innocents of life. One less threat to the safety of his brother.

He'd deteriorated into a laughable monster, though, drinking from criminals, resorting once to a few of the park's fowl and night mammals. When was the last time he stooped so low? A century ago, at least. Now, with Marie no doubt a few days or weeks at most from ending his existence, he thought of his whole life, barely remembering the time before mother flew at him in a frenzy and took his soul. Had he been happy before then? Had he done anything worthwhile?

No, he'd been a worthless mortal as well. A failure, with one exception. He'd helped a mortal woman escape an asylum, and he'd pushed her onto a path she might otherwise never have taken. What had she done since? Re-indulged her dangerous drug habit? Gone back to her fantasies? Been locked up again? Or had he truly made a difference? He had to know.

Why, George? What will you do when you find out?

She'd asked him to stay a while, but he'd fled more quickly because of it. Not for his sake, but for hers. And now?

He didn't know what to expect, what to do. But he would see her again, even if from the shadows, to make sure she was well. And then he would let Marie do her worst. It was probably far past time. He tired of running. He would stand and fight, and lose, for Marie was powerful and had a large and lethal following. George had no one. He made a mental note to write a letter to Phillip, who would no doubt take on supreme responsibility and guilt for failing to protect him. That wouldn't do at all. Let the better brother have a few good years with a lovely wife.

The Altamont Hotel had unfortunately not changed in a week—had it only been a week? With the chill of fall starting to take hold, smoke curled from most chimneys. The night auditor nodded blandly as George signed the register under another alias and pocketed the key. This time he'd take a large suite on the top floor, still with a view of Eutaw Street below. He'd have to be a bit more careful in his approach to Lillian. It wouldn't do to creep onto her balcony again.

George sighed and lit his pipe, stared into the fire and thought of her, hair fanned out across her pillow, white gown hugging her lovely form.

CHAPTER SEVENTEEN

Coming and going.

The Musketeers lined up by height, wiggling in anticipation of treats and pennies, and Lillian folded her arms behind her back and paced in front of them.

Her nerves sizzled as she waited for any news of Madam Pelosi. The Orleanses' butler had reported that Phillip, Kitty, and Annaluisa had left on a train for a destination he didn't know. Lillian knew he lied—he knew where they had gone—but had stopped short of pleading with him. No, she'd instead sent the boys on a mission to scour the city for any sign of the trio's whereabouts. Bess had visited the Langhan sisters to find clues, and to make gentle inquiries about the identity of the mysterious disappearance of a socialite twenty-four years earlier. They'd been no help, however; she had no doubt simply aroused the gossiping nature of Etta Langhan.

"Yes, Darby? What do you have for me?"

The boy pulled his cap off and rubbed at his nose, stalling. "I heard they're gone, all of them Orleanses, and the lady artist and the lady with the veils."

"We knew that, Darby." He looked like he might cry, so she ruffled his hair and pressed a penny into his palm. "Billy, did you do better?"

Billy toed the ground and shook his head. "Paddy stole my idea. I told him they might still be at the train station, and so he went there. It ain't fair, is it, Miss? Him taking my idea?"

Good Lord, why didn't I think of that? "A penny for your idea. So did you go, Paddy? Did you learn anything?"

"I didn't see them about, but I saw the brother." Paddy turned and punched Billy. "Wasn't your idea, was *our* idea."

"Paddy, stop that! Are you sure it was Mr. Phillip's brother?"

"I'm sure."

Lillian clasped her hands more tightly to stop them from shaking. *George.* He'd gone far away, never to be seen again. Her heart sank as she realized what Paddy had witnessed: He'd simply come back to Baltimore to say goodbye to his brother before leaving for good.

"You saw him board a train, Paddy? Do you know where it was going?"

"Is 'board' going or coming?"

"Going."

"He was coming. Got off the train."

"You are certain? He got off the train in Baltimore?"

"We're in Baltimore, Miss Holmes."

"Right. And being a bright boy, you followed him, didn't you?"

Paddy rolled his eyes. "A course. I hopped the back of his cab. I'm good at that."

"So dangerous, Paddy! Hasn't Aileen talked to you about doing that?" Bess scolded.

Lillian sent her friend a look. "He obviously survived. So, Paddy, where did he go?"

Paddy pointed across the street and down the block. "That place, the hotel."

"The Hotel Altamont? Are you very sure?" Paddy nodded, but she barely saw him, her vision blurring. She sat, overwhelmed with need to see him again. Why had he returned? *You will not cry. This is one of the symptoms; George warned you it might happen.*

Bess paid Paddy, shoed the boys away, and joined her. "You love him."

"Of course not."

"Yes, you do. Or something quite close to it. I have never seen that expression on your face. I am not a woman of the world, and I don't know much about men, but I know you. And my guess is that he has come back for you. When he came to ask me to help him free you from Spring Grove, I saw a man obsessed. With you."

"I don't know up from down right now, Bess. My thoughts and feelings are a jumble."

"You are different, Lil. Life is no longer a game to you. I see it. George Orleans has a hand in this change."

"True."

"While I don't think it wise to trust him, I believe he might help you further. I can speak to him if you are afraid."

Bess shook her foot, and Lillian snickered. "You would brave the jungle beast for me?"

"Stop treating me like that! It's most unfair. I will take your pistol."

"No, I'll go. I am afraid to see him again, but not because I fear he'll kill me."

"I understand."

Bess squeezed her hand, and Lillian realized her friend did understand.

"Take me with you, at least?"

"No. This I must do for myself."

Within two hours Lillian had finished writing in her Journal of Important Observations, with notations about George Orleans should things go amiss at the Hotel Altamont. She also penned notes to Addie, Thomas, and Aileen, thanking them for their love and support. A letter was addressed to Mr. Francis Pemberton, Esq., notifying him that he was no longer in the service of her estate. She did not mention her hatred of him, that she considered him the devil himself. And she copied her letter to Pemberton word for word and addressed it to a second lawyer, Bess's cousin, Richard Wheeler, whom she'd met the previous day. He would ensure her wishes were followed.

She put on the emerald silk Aileen had purchased that very day, which had yet to be altered, fixed her own hair, and loaded her pistol. After pressing a kiss to the letter from Mr. Conan Doyle, she left her room, left the security of her home, which had indeed felt like a prison these many years, and strode up the street toward the Altamont. As she walked, she rehearsed her speech for George should he be there.

I am here to inquire about my mother because I believe you may have information on her. If you do not, will you at least tell me the whereabouts of Annaluisa? I am ready for her message. Thank you for your help.

Her stomach churned. At best, she would not betray her confused feelings for him and he would be able to tell her something. At worst, he would kill her because she knew his hand in two murders. As she took the stairs to the hotel entrance, she was no longer sure she'd weighed the equation properly.

The clerk inclined his head and smiled. "I believe I've seen you before, Miss. You are a resident of this neighborhood, correct?"

"Yes, I've walked by here many times. But today I am looking for one of your guests. A Mr. George Orleans."

The clerk ran his finger down the register and shook his head. "No, I'm afraid not, Miss. Perhaps he will check in tomorrow?"

Lillian asked him to try again, and looked with him. She caught her breath. "There! I'm very sorry, how silly. I am to see a Mr. Lestrade, not Orleans. Orleans is the cousin."

"Ah! Wonderful. I will have the bellman deliver a message for you, if you would take a seat."

"I'd rather go myself."

The welcoming smile turned dour. "It's rather late."

"Nevertheless, I will see him now." *Go ahead, think what you like.*

"The fifth floor, suite B, Miss."

Ignoring the brand-new elevator, Lillian climbed the curved staircase, each step making her heart pound in terror of what she might find. How would he receive her?

As she reached the fifth-floor landing, she checked the empty hallway and patted her pistol secure in her waistcoat. She straightened the dagger strapped to her wrist, and willing her hand to stop shaking she knocked on the door of suite B.

"It is unlocked. Enter," a voice called from within. George.

Perhaps he's expecting someone? A lover? Lillian turned the handle and opened the door a few inches. "It is Miss Holmes. May I come in?"

He pulled the door open and stared at her in shock. "Good Lord, how did you find me? *Why* did you find me?"

He wore a simple heavy black dressing robe over his night pants, exposing a good deal of neck and chest. Barefooted and disheveled, he narrowed his eyes at her silence.

The churning in her gut changed in an instant. She feared him, but she desired him more.

Sensing that he could read could read her longing on her face, she peered past him into the room and took a deep breath. "I have my methods, Mr. Lestrade."

"Goodness, is that the name I used?" He rubbed at the stubble on his chin. "You must have been on my mind at the time. I wanted to come visit you, to see how you fared, but I also did not want to frighten you again by approaching through your window. I... I..."

He shook his head and motioned for her to enter and sit. When she hesitated, he pulled her by the hand to the settee. Only a single lamp lit the large suite. Lillian found it comforting, found it too easy to be with George again. Her speech forgotten, she took in the scent of him, spicy and exotic, and tried to pull her gaze away from his lips and sad, deep chocolate-colored eyes.

"You look forlorn, George. It is not what I expected."

"What did you expect?" He brushed his fingers along her jaw and she clutched at them to stop his caress. She could barely think in his presence; his touch made it impossible.

"Some devil-may-care shenanigans, perhaps. Why are you not in your home? Is something amiss?"

He blew out a breath and propped his bare feet on the table. "It is not your problem. Let us just say that I am awaiting an inevitable meeting."

"With the police?"

"How I wish. No, an old enemy who wishes to harm me. That is why you must leave. You may become a casualty in that petty war."

"I see." Lillian nodded. George would not share his secret life with her even though he knew hers.

"No, you don't. You know nothing about me, except for a few facts you choose to ignore because I helped you escape the asylum."

"That is not it."

"I am not your savior, Lil. You look well. You look wonderful, beautiful." He held her gaze and then lowered his eyes to her lips, to her neck. "Do not confuse me with a normal man interested in your health and happiness."

"No, I know you are not a normal man."

He sat up straight and pulled his hand away. So, it was all true. He *was* hiding something, something extraordinary. "Are you ready to confess that you are a murderer?"

"Not in the sense you mean. But I have caused great pain, suffering…and yes, death."

"And do you enjoy causing these things?"

He seemed to seriously contemplate her question, his brow furrowed. "Enjoy? Why, I suppose I have enjoyed it, yes. I've always thought of it as more of a need, as you have needed your 'medicine.' But at times I've gone far past need into enjoyment. At most times, in fact. I…"

"You are enjoying it less. Is that correct?"

He nodded. "Something like that. I'm tired, Lil. You…you remind me so much of myself when I was…younger. I wasn't so ordinary, ever. I didn't fit in like Phillip did. People didn't warm to me. They thought me daft at times. Excessive, brash, impulsive, even irrational. Nothing, and no one, held my attention for more than an hour. But it was better than what I have become. That is why I'm allowing my enemy to find me."

"How old are you, George? You said I remind you of yourself when you were younger, but in truth, we look about the same age. That is far from reality, is it not?"

He hooded his eyes and shrugged with a deep sigh. "It is a painful topic, and one that defies logic. Please don't trouble yourself over it. In any case, this life is nearly over."

"You would give up? After convincing me to push on and live my life to the fullest?"

"There's nothing left for me. I have no family except Phillip, and I'll no longer put his happiness at risk. I have no friends. I'm tired and bored and more than a bit angry at myself for how I've wasted my life."

"I don't see how we are different now. Except that you are not following your advice to me. You are not choosing to live."

"For what? You can't understand, and I am not able to make you understand. Please leave, Lil, before it's too late. I came back to make sure you were sound. I don't want to have gone to all that trouble merely to have you killed at the Hotel Altamont."

"You came back for me, and yet…"

"Yes, and yet. It cannot be."

Can I love a man who hates himself? It doesn't matter, he does not want me.

"Then I will leave you. May I ask if you know the whereabouts of my mother, or failing that, the name of someone who might lead me to her?"

George smiled, and Lillian's heart broke. She knew she'd not be likely to see that beautiful smile again.

"You are formidable, Miss Holmes." He threw his arm around her and pulled her in for what felt like a brotherly hug. She wanted to slap him, it felt so awful.

"My mother's name and whereabouts, please?"

"I don't know. But Madam Annaluisa Pelosi does. Unfortunately, it seems she has fled Baltimore with Phil and Kitty, and I'm not sure where they went. Likely back to New Orleans. I'll wager that they will return before long, and you'll be able to question Annaluisa in person. She was willing to help once. I'm sure she will again."

"Then I won't trouble you any longer."

Lillian wanted to stand, tried to stand, but she couldn't make her muscles respond. George seemed to note her hesitation. He turned her chin so that she faced him, and angled his face an inch from hers. His breath sent a chill across her soul, his deep eyes turned midnight black. He put his hand around her neck and sent ice-cold shivers down her back with the rub of his thumb.

"I am your worst enemy, Lil. If I did not care for you... If I did not want you so badly I'd consider living this bleak life a while longer, I would ask you to stay."

"Ask me," she whispered. "Can we not feel bleak together? I would dearly love your help now."

"Eventually I would be the death of you."

"I do not believe it. You have had every opportunity to kill me."

"You cannot know what you're saying."

She closed the distance between them and pressed her lips to his. He resisted for a heart-stopping second, and then he fell into her with a hunger she didn't know possible. As he claimed her mouth again and again, she heard herself moaning and the quiet hiss of her name from his lips. His skin was cold, so cold, and his eyes so dark, she felt as if she were freezing into his world inch by inch as he tossed aside her hat and loosened her chignon. He clutched her hair in one hand and yanked her head back so that he could kiss her neck.

If she'd ever dreamed of passion before, the memory disappeared beneath his demanding lips. A nick at her neck and she gasped, sensations pouring through her whole body, pooling in hot-cold spirals to her womb.

He groaned and pressed his lips to hers again, but he now tasted of blood, of *her* blood. Tangy. When she reached her hand to her neck, he whimpered and pushed it behind her back.

"I am sorry. It will not happen again."

"Is this the preamble to murder, this nick upon my neck?"

"No, not with you. It is a lust to taste all of you... How can I explain? All my desires blend into one. But you are safe." He ripped her waistcoat away and leaned back, staring at the pistol tucked in her skirt band. "Might we remove that for now? I will return it to you."

Looking into his eyes, Lillian believed him. She pulled the pistol free and put it on the table next to the settee. Then she reached up her sleeve and removed the slender dagger she wore.

George narrowed his eyes and shook his head. Then smiled. "Anything else I need to know about?"

"My diary names you as my killer should I not return home."

"Splendid. How much time do we have before they come looking for you?"

"At least a year."

She slid her hand down his chest and brushed the smooth skin with her palms. With a growl, he picked her up and carried her to the bedroom. He threw his nightgown onto the floor and knelt next to her, a pale muscular marble statue, chest heaving with effort as he tore layer after layer of clothing off of her.

"Aileen will be angry; this dress is new."

"Shut up and help me."

When she was down to her corset, he fell on her, licking an icy hot path down her neck and, after freeing her breasts from the tight fabric, licking and suckling on her nipples. This was not the ardor of her fantasies. It was better. This man would tear her apart, inch by inch, and she would beg him to do it again. She arched against his mouth and cried his name, raking her nails across his back and pleading for more, for less, for mercy as his touches sent lightning to her sex and thunder in her ears.

"Tell me you want this," he whispered as he ran his palm down her stomach and ripped her bloomers away. "Tell me you need this, that I don't frighten you."

"You do frighten me. And I want this, I want you." She tensed for a moment, remembering a night in which she was young, naked, and frightened, when no one asked or cared what she wanted. This man, *this* man cared. She pushed down the past and blew out the breath she was holding.

"This is so cruel." He brought her hand to his stomach, and she ran it down the cords of muscle along his hips. She found her prize, thick and hard with urgent need. As she ran her palm over the slick head, he cried out and then took her in a kiss again.

She ran her hand along the shaft, tentatively at first, then in long, hard strokes that seemed to please him most, and he bucked and nipped at her neck. Another tiny nick—she felt it—and he backed away.

"I'm so sorry, Lil. The taste of you, it draws me, it overwhelms me..."

"I will be wearing high collars this winter," she joked. *But God, is it true? He wants my neck more than my womanhood?*

George pulled away and stared into her eyes. "I am damaged, my love. I am not sure of myself. You are everything... You don't know..."

"We are all damaged, George. Please, please do not stop now."

"Forgive me, then, for I was always a selfish man."

He tore the rest of her clothes away and stripped himself fully naked, a beautiful man with fire in his eyes. She brushed his overlong hair from his face as he hovered over her, and she watched as his irises and pupils blended to black. Slowly at first, he pressed himself into her, and when she stretched to receive him, he built a slick fire with a steady rhythm that sent sparks through her veins. She watched him as long as she could keep her eyes open, watched the greed and need on his wondrous face. When she had to close her eyes as sensations drowned her and stars exploded in the darkness, she heard his hiss and whispered curse. He fell on her finally and said her name.

She nestled against his chest and held on, knowing that like everyone else who mattered, he would be taken away from her as well. Willing herself not to cry, she wondered what she would wear home. Hopefully her skirt was in one piece.

CHAPTER EIGHTEEN

A hint of better times.

In silence, George retrieved his robe and moved to the sitting room, giving Lillian time to wash and dress as best she could. He regretted the interlude, regretted ever having met her. Didn't she feel the same? It was *not* better to have lusted and lost. Especially in the space of a few days.

Why should he not feel sated now? No, his hunger intensified by the moment, both for her blood and her sex. No, for all of her. To own her, to own her forever.

Why not, then? *Take her, turn her, keep her!* But he knew he wouldn't, and he wondered if he'd ever understand why.

***

"Get on with it, Lil," she thought. "You have survived worse. You have mysteries to solve." The mystery of her mother, the mystery of her stolen child. If only she had a bottle of small pills to calm her nerves, but no, that would be choosing a different kind of death. Better to die a little bit at a time and let Providence take its natural course.

George tapped at the bedroom door and put her pistol, dagger, hat, and boots on the dresser. "Are you well?"

His broad smile mocked the dread she felt. Could he be *that* uncaring, to not know that he had moved her body and soul? Of course, hadn't he claimed a tryst with her neighbor? And how many other neighbors? He had told her he was her worst enemy. Perhaps he had been telling the truth.

"I am quite well, sir. I will join you in a moment."

"I was thinking we might have dinner tomorrow…somewhere discreet. If my enemy has not found me. Would you consider that?" Then he left her to finish dressing.

The uncertainty in his voice thrilled her. How out of character. Could he have been moved? No, he wanted another coupling, that was all. *And what do you want, Lillian Holmes?* Certainly not a man with so many secrets that he could not be trusted. But it squeezed at her heart, the realization that she did want someone. Not a fortune-seeker like Aloysius Hoyt but a man who would not want her to change, who would forgive her oddities, absolve her of the shame of her past addiction and help keep her on the straight and narrow, and who would accept her child, should she be able to find her. No, she wanted a man to help her find her daughter, to help raise her as his own. She wanted to be loved. *It is a tall order,* she thought.

"Oh, and passion!" she added to herself. Not the quick encounter she'd just had with George. They hadn't truly shared passion. For he did not love her, and she did not love him. They were simply two odd creatures thrown together by God for an unfathomable purpose. George Orleans had given her that gift of need and desire. Perhaps that was reason enough.

What had she given him? Forgiveness? Forbearance? At least he didn't languish in a prison for assaulting her. Yet, had it truly felt like an assault? No, it had felt like the oddest of courtships.

He was in the next room, and yet he felt a million miles away. She smelled him on her clothes, felt the aftereffects of their coupling; her lips still tingled from his kisses. But he would remain a mystery, and he would leave her again. There seemed no question of that.

She finished dressing and steeled herself for seeing his handsome face again, his penetrating eyes, his lips either quirked up in a smile or pressed tightly together for whatever pain he kept inside. He waited for her, pacing, tall and stately, elegant long fingers pushing through his disheveled hair.

Lillian stood in the bedroom doorway, staring transfixed as he turned and stared at her. "The Leaping Man," she whispered. "I wish I understood the Leaping Man."

"I understand him less at this moment than ever before."

"You were to be my first case, the first criminal to be locked up, taken away from society because of my sleuthing. Instead, I now begin another case. I will find my child and learn about my mother. I have my wits, and perhaps my health. The city no longer wants my demise."

"And what of your Uncle Sherlock? Must you release that fantasy as well? What a shame. I found it rather endearing."

Lillian laughed, the sound nearly foreign to her ears. She lifted her chin and smiled. "How do you know it's not true? Are you so certain that there isn't a real Sherlock Holmes somewhere?"

"Fairly certain. At least not by that name."

"I rather think I'll still call him Uncle. He has served me well these few years. I cannot tolerate the thought of being completely normal."

"I don't think you need worry about that."

His sad smile silenced her retort. So, this was the end, and they both knew it.

"Don't let your enemy find you. Leave now. I am well. You needn't ever worry about me. Don't let me spend my days worried about you. Perhaps you will send me a letter and tell me of your escapades, my Leaping Man. I will tell you about my cases, and you can advise me from afar."

"Lil." His voice broke, and he turned away.

"Go, go then. I wish you trusted me enough to let me help you as you have helped me. But never mind that, I know you will not. Flee this city before it swallows you as it once wanted to swallow me. Go to a place where it is safe to be a vampire."

He opened his mouth in shock, then closed it and stared into her eyes for a long moment. "Then you understand why I leave you. I have enjoyed our short friendship. If I had anything to offer God, I would trade it for a chance to...have more time with you."

Lillian thought her chest would burst. What to do? What to say? Did he truly mean it? Yes, she saw it in his eyes, and she knew finally what she wanted.

"This would seem the right time to ask if I'd flee with you, George. A sane woman would not entertain the idea, but the niece of Sherlock Holmes craves adventure, and, although she does not easily admit it, companionship. Or, if you prefer, we could fight your enemy together, here. I could enlist...well, Bess would be willing, and Constable Moran surely would help if the cause were just. Also your brother, Kitty, Annaluisa...you are not alone. The woman is called Marie? How could one woman compete against us all? Especially given your particular talent for draining mortals of their life blood."

He fell into the armchair and put his hands over his face. Through his fingers he whispered, "Do you love me, Lillian?"

It was a startling question, as was the answer. "I rather think I do."

"Knowing what you know?"

He looked at her now, and she took a step back, shocked at a trickle of blood on his cheek as he shed a red tear, his eyes scarlet-tinted in an unnatural way. Her hands shook and her nerves sprang to life. Still, she held her ground.

"Do you love what you see now? How ugly am I to you? Do you know what it is to commit unthinkable acts on a daily basis with no remorse?" His skin grew even paler, and a dark vein surfaced on his temple.

"While I am unaccustomed to seeing this change, it is not totally unexpected. And I do hear remorse in your voice."

"Blazes, woman! Leave now! Don't you understand? Before I change my mind and drain the life from your body! Go!"

Lillian took a seat across from him. How certain was she of her love? Well, she hadn't truly lived before she met him, so would she lose so much? "No, I won't go, not unless you tell me you do not love me."

"I do not love you."

His words didn't sting, as his voice shook and he would not meet her gaze. "Nonsense. You are trying to protect me...from a vampire. I did read Mr. Stoker's new novel. I thought it complete fiction, but then, they say that truth is stranger than fiction."

"You know nothing about it."

"Of course, I was not convinced at first, but then I remembered Mr. Holmes's rule."

"What?"

"When you have eliminated the impossible, whatever remains, however improbable, must be the truth. I must say, this situation has tested my definitions of impossible and improbable. I have believed it for quite a while." Lillian stood and reached her hand down to George. "So, which will it be? Will you kill me now, will you stay and fight with my assistance, or shall we flee Baltimore?"

He took her hand and stood, and brushed away a bloody tear. "It would never be safe for you. My kind will always find me, and that makes your safety impossible. If one of them...changed you, Lillian, I could not bear it. It's a dreadful life, one that defies description. You would hate it, you would hate me. I cannot guarantee you will be protected from that, although I would do my best..."

"I know," she said. The words meant everything.

"I love you so much," he whispered.

"I know."

George pulled her in so tightly he squeezed the air from her lungs, but he breathed life back into her with his demanding kiss. He pulled away and, holding her close, spoke as if to himself. "I don't deserve this moment of happiness. It cannot be true."

"Do remember Mr. Holmes's rule, George."

His laughter melted her heart, and he kissed her again.

CHAPTER NINETEEN

Lillian finds her nemesis.

George snickered as he packed his things, wondering how Lillian would take to the Wild West. She was home collecting her belongings.

He'd spent an hour ignoring the pulls at his conscience and allowed himself a feeling so rare he barely remembered ever having experienced it: joy. He laughed again at himself, at his infatuation. No, *obsession,* he corrected. Only an hour or so, and he'd be in her company again. He'd never let her out of his sight. Of course, he had to find a way to defeat Marie and eventually return to Baltimore, sooner rather than later, for Lil still had to find her daughter. And they needed to find Annaluisa to learn about her mother. If what he remembered of his brief conversation on the subject was correct, he'd have to prepare Lillian for the second shocking truth: Her mother was not quite dead.

How would this all work? The worry was just under the surface, and he struggled to push it down. What would she say when he had to feed, had to kill? How had Phillip managed? *Damn it, why isn't he here? I would speak with Kitty as well.*

The urgent banging on his door startled him. *No, not Marie, not now!* Then again, Marie would likely not come crashing into his hotel room. She would have less obvious ways of removing him.

"Mr. Orleans, please answer!"

The Wheeler woman. George ran to the door and pulled Bess inside. His heart dropped at the state of her. Perspiration beaded on her forehead, her hair was disheveled, and her eyes showed signs of recent tears.

"What has happened to Lil?" He clutched the young woman by the shoulders and had to resist shaking her for an answer.

Bess struggled to catch her breath as he helped her to a chair. "I came as quickly as I could. I am slow with my foot—"

"You did the right thing. Tell me!"

"They are there, the Jackal and Dr. Schneider. I know they mean to lock her away again. They want to dismiss Thomas and Addie, have already thrown Aileen and her brothers out onto the street. Lil was arguing with them when I arrived. I am sure now they want her money and not her health! I never liked Pemberton, but I thought the doctor... Never mind that now. Go, please help her!"

George pulled on his overcoat and loaded a pistol he kept for just such occasions. He caught Bess's wide-eyed stare. "It will be all right. Hopefully they won't force me to kill them." *Though I'm unlikely to do it with this.*

"Oh, I hope you do!" The girl's face was grimmer than he imagined it had ever been. "I was wondering if you have another weapon that I could use?"

"Lil would not forgive me if you were to be hurt. Please go to your home, and I'll be sure to send word."

Bess looked mournful. "I could not keep up with you in any case. I would gladly accept this grotesque limp for the rest of my life if this one day I could move quickly to help you!"

George squeezed her hand. "You have already done magnificently." Then he rushed out the door, terror squeezing his heart.

Lillian's residence seemed quiet when he arrived, with a light burning only in the front parlor. A cab with the marking of a hospital was pulled up close; a largish-looking man was strolling up and down before its horses.

Yes, they meant to take her away. He would find entry into her home through the alleyway.

***

Just the sight of the Jackal made Lillian's skin crawl and her stomach twist. When had she last been near him? Only once or twice since that night so many years ago, and she had denied herself that memory. His soft fat hands laced together over his girth, his greasy hair now thinned and his nose now bulbous, no doubt from drink. The years had not been kind to a man who was ugly to begin with.

And now, clearly, a second betrayal unfolded.

"How long have you been in the employ of this man, Dr. Schneider? Since I was sixteen or so?"

A flash of confusion across his face gave her hope. "Lillian, we are friends. I am concerned for you."

"Whatever this man has told you is a lie. He is after my inheritance. I am as sane as you."

"My dear, the fantasies have returned, the elixirs… You need help."

"I am *not* delusional. I am damaged, perhaps, but that was not my doing. Until an hour ago, I was actually happy for the first time in my life. That was not your doing, not Francis Pemberton's. Once again, you are dismissed. Both of you. I have retained new counsel, and he will see to my affairs shortly. His name is Wheeler."

The men exchanged a quick glance, and Lillian's heart sank. She would attempt to flee, but she knew they would stop her. She screamed in anger and impotent rage. Were Addie and Thomas still in the house? It seemed not. She was so alone, so totally alone, in the hands of two men who had helped destroy her life.

Would George come again to the asylum, free her again, take her far away where the monsters could not follow? No, this time they would see to it that she didn't live long. Looking into Francis

Pemberton's eyes she was certain he would never let her assume independence over her estate, would never risk the truth of his crime be exposed. No, he saw he had lost control over her. And he would likely kill her rather than relinquish her fortune.

"I only had one day with him," she murmured. "You gave me only one day."

Dr. Schneider sighed. "You see, Lillian, you are babbling again. You never should have left Spring Grove; you still require serious help."

The Jackal turned on the doctor. "Can you assure me that she will not escape again? How could you have been so remiss?"

"I have told you, she must have had assistance. She was not strong enough to find her way back to the city."

The Jackal faced Lillian. "A Spring Grove employee is right outside the house, Miss Holmes. I left him there hoping to avoid a scene. Should I call him in to restrain you, or will you come willingly?"

She stared at the Jackal, anger boiling in her veins. "Do not speak to me again, unless it is to tell me where my daughter is."

"Daughter? Why, you have no daughter. Another delusion. How sad," the lawyer said in a mocking tone.

"You will burn in hell for what you did to me. I was a girl! You forced yourself on me and then you ripped my baby away! You had me drugged into silence, threatened to kill me should I reveal your true nature. I hate you! You took everything from me, and now you would have my home, my inheritance? I will not allow it!" *Please, God, let me have one more day with George. Someone help me.*

Pemberton scowled and turned to the doctor. "We tried your way. Wheeler will investigate, and all shall come to light. We must make sure she can never speak again."

Schneider nodded.

So, then, the doctor, too? After all these years, so many confidences... Lillian ran her hand down to her pocket, not willing to let them lay a hand on her again.

Her fingers had just touched the metal of her pistol when she heard the pop of a gun and felt a sting in her chest. Her legs folded under her, and she thought of George, hoped he would choose life even though hers was done. The last thing she heard was Addie's scream, a male voice, and two more gunshots.

***

George leaned against the wall and watched as an older woman dressed like a governess hugged the lifeless body of Lillian to her chest, rocking her as if she were a baby, howling in pain, covered in her blood.

A tall elderly man stood next to her, face buried in his hands, frail body shaking as he wept. "Is she gone?" he mumbled through his hands.

The woman nodded through her cries.

Dead? Lillian was dead? Numbly George thought it would be nice if he himself could be killed by a single bullet.

The man Lillian said raped her twitched on the floor, one of the two men George had shot—too late. He stood straight, walked on weak legs to the man's side, and shot him again, this time in the face. The burly hospital cab driver rushed in from outside, no doubt having heard the ruckus, and George shot him at point-blank range. Then he dropped the pistol, stepped over the body of the driver and walked out of the house forever.

CHAPTER TWENTY

A monster's prayer.

George knew not where he'd go. Perhaps he'd simply keep walking, not stop to feed, and let nature take its course. How long would it be? Not long perhaps, if he let the sun weaken him. No matter, he thought. It wasn't a bad plan at all.

"Are you George?" He'd taken only a few steps and turned to see Lillian's old butler waving to him from her porch. "She is asking for you!"

"Pardon?"

"Hurry!"

George leapt up and past the man into the parlor. The scene had not changed, but the woman holding Lillian looked to him, agony etched across her face.

"You are George? She said your name more than once. I thought her dead, but she spoke your name…"

George knelt down and put his ear to Lillian's chest. A mortal would not be able to hear the faint murmur within, but he did. "Lil. Lil, can you hear me?"

She did not respond.

"Leave us," he instructed. The old pair stood still. "If you ever loved her, leave us now! Leave the house and do not come back until I send word! Is anyone else about?"

The man shook his head.

"Lock the door behind you!"

The two rose and obeyed. He could see in their face that there was no hope, that they would give everything to take back what had just happened. As would George.

As their sobbing grew faint, he stared down into Lillian's white face. He pressed his lips to hers and whispered, "Love, it's me."

Her eyes fluttered open, flicked around, glazed, and he searched for any sign of the incomparable woman within. Yes, there was recognition. He pressed on her wound and she groaned.

What to do? There was only one option. He could not choose for her, but was she strong enough to understand? Should he even offer her this life of damnation? Didn't every vampire spawn hate their maker at some point? He could not bear it if she hated him.

Oh, please, Lil, please!

"It is a harsh, miserable existence, but it is an existence, Lil. Quickly, do you want to stay?" *God in heaven, if you can hear the prayer of a monster, hear mine.*

She closed her eyes again, and he stopped breathing. *Please, please, please.*

"Yes," she croaked. "You. My baby…yes."

George took a breath and prayed again that it wasn't too late. She needed strength to drink. He ripped at his wrist with his teeth and held it to her mouth. She didn't move, but he opened her lips so a few drops could get in.

It's not enough! This fasting has left me too weak!

He sucked from his own wrist and put his mouth to hers, spat the blood into her. She coughed and protested but swallowed. He repeated the process three times as he caressed her hair and coaxed her. She drank a little more each time, and her eyes gradually seemed to gain awareness.

And now…

George scanned the parlor and found a letter opener on the desk, closed his eyes and plunged it into his neck. Lillian stared at him, repulsion in her eyes, but she did as he said when he lifted her to nestle against his neck. Her warm tongue ran along his skin, and he held her tightly, bidding her to drink. And drink she did.

She grew stronger, and he ran his hand through the blood pooled on her chest, pressing it to his mouth and licking her life into his own. Nothing in his existence had prepared him for the sense that he was now complete. He'd given life, such as it was, to someone who loved him. He hoped she'd still love him when she understood the full bargain.

The strain was too much. He'd given her too much too fast. But just before he passed into unconsciousness, he clung to Lillian tightly, telling her how he loved her and thanking God for hearing a monster.

CHAPTER TWENTY-ONE

The Leaping Woman.

"Come join us, Lil," George chided. He rubbed her shoulders and leaned in to kiss her neck, and his icy breath sent a thrill up Lillian's spine to mix with the euphoria he assured her would pass.

As it would be a crisis purportedly to "make her recovery from morphine addiction seem like the bite of an ant," Lillian hoped the transition would be complete before Annaluisa returned from New Orleans, where she'd apparently gone to spread rumors of George's departure to the west. Madam Lucifer and her minions would be put off the scent for a while, he and his brother Phillip believed, but that wouldn't last long, for the woman was far too clever to commit all her resources in one direction. Too, Lillian grew breathless whenever she imagined asking Annaluisa's return. She could soon ask about her mother! The truth was so close.

For a week she'd spent half her time drinking the blood George provided, without questioning its origin, and hungering for more. The other half was spent in his arms, naked, learning how naïve her fantasies had been, how the reality of George's sexual appetites defied description. The best part of surviving the Jackal, besides the knowledge that he could no longer hurt her, was living to see George smile and laugh and enjoy himself. They were as one, and she enjoyed the ties that bound them. He'd warned her that she would come to resent him as her maker, but she didn't believe that. She could never resent him. He'd saved her life more than once.

They had managed to return her house to some normalcy within a week. The three deaths were explained away as the work of a vicious burglar who caught Lillian's visitors unaware. Lillian and those in her employ were said to have escaped in the nick of time through the rear of the house. Thank God that the children were not about, the neighbors commented.

Aileen and her fortunate brothers were now reinstalled in the household. Addie and Thomas posed a more difficult problem, but after briefly seeing Lillian they had been convinced finally that she was recuperating and needed quiet solitude. At George's suggestion, Lillian bought the Wheeler seaside cottage and sent Thomas and Addie for a long-overdue holiday. Perhaps they could stay there, she considered, though she would miss them.

And, what to do about Bess? The loss of her dear friend haunted her day and night, and was a thorn on the rose of her new life with her love. After *almost* convincing George and Phillip that Bess knew nothing of import about them, which was a bit of a lie, George had urged her to put the matter aside.

"I am so sorry, love. This kind of loss is common, nay, inevitable. It is best for her; you must try to keep your focus on that."

"I do not think she would tell others about us, George, if I were to tell her the truth."

He had shaken his head in pity. "If there were a governing House in Baltimore, she might be dead already, Lil. The more distance you put between yourself and Bess, the safer we are, the safer she is. I will not hurt her, but Madam Lucifer would not care about your feelings for her, nor would others of our kind."

"Then I must abandon my home, Aileen and the boys, Thomas and Addie as well?"

"We will speak of this, on how you must behave, on what care you must take. And do not forget that when the hunger is upon you, one of those little boys will look like a very tempting snack."

She'd wept in his arms at having lost so much for this chance to live. She'd had so little to begin with.

Bess had come calling early in the week to check on her, and she'd begged George to let them speak. He had. They'd all dined together, and then Bess pulled Lillian into the parlor for a private talk. She'd grilled Lillian on the details of the deaths of the Jackal, doctor, and the driver. While she'd seemed accepting of the truth of their demises, she'd looked unconvinced by Lillian's answers regarding her recovery.

"You trust George, do you not, Bess? You are the one who ran to him—who saved me, in truth! It was a very happy circumstance that he was able to nurse me back from the edge of death. He is very knowledgeable."

Bess jutted her chin out. "While I am your intellectual inferior, Lil, you do me a great disservice. My disfigurement has not addled my brain. I heard talk of vampires, of strange occurrences. What I see with my own eyes is some change in your person. *Tell me what has happened.*"

"I cannot, Bess. It is for your safety—"

"No." Her friend was upset. "Why are the Orleans brothers so strange? What of Kitty? You all speak a secret language without words, by looks and signals and nods. I know George saved your life and that I am the one who asked him to, but—"

"And I am grateful to you. Please trust me. More I cannot say. Perhaps in due course..."

"I thought you were finished with secrets, Lil! I was to be your Miss Watson. I suppose I am no longer needed as you have your George. I have encountered such a dismissal more than once: Once betrothed, a friend serves less purpose." Bess shrugged and wiped away tears. "Perhaps I would be no better if the situation were reversed. But I always thought you nobler than any woman I knew."

Lillian bit her lip lest a scarlet tear escape and draw more scrutiny from Bess, but her heart felt crushed. "We still have to search for my mother and baby. And I have not forgotten that finding you a husband is on my life list. Oh, Bess, I love you so. I wish I could speak freely."

"If you will not speak freely, then I think we cannot be friends—and that your love is rather weak." With that, Bess had stood and quit the house, leaving Lillian alive but with a brand-new hole in her heart.

Phillip and Kitty sat now at a table, the latter sketching with charcoal while Phillip read.

"I'll join you in a moment, Georgy," Lillian said, glancing up at him hovering over her shoulder. "I've wanted to write my friend for a while. Give me a moment."

"Your friend?" George frowned. "Lil, do you feel well? To which friend are you referring?"

She smiled. "I am quite well. Have no fear that I am imagining him or our correspondence, or that I am giving away any particular secrets. We have talked, and I will show you proof tonight."

She winked, and George kissed her hand and joined his brother at the table.

Dear Mr. Conan Doyle,

I hope this finds you well. Perhaps you'll remember that we corresponded a few years ago about my namesake, or so I like to think of Mr. Sherlock Holmes. You were so kind in encouraging me to pursue my desire of becoming like your great detective, and you advised me to take great care. I likely should have heeded that warning a bit more.

I am writing to report that I have solved my first case, although in a somewhat circuitous fashion. I trust further investigations will go more smoothly. You noted correctly in your letter to me that it might bring sadness to know there is no real Holmes family in your circle. Indeed, I have lived as an orphan but have recently learned that two of my relatives may be alive. That will be my next case, and I am happy to report that I am surrounded by good friends whom I believe will assist me. Indeed, one of those friends is my new beau! He is smart and has a rather dry sense of humor, and he reminds me somehow of your great hero, with a few important differences. But enough about my personal life.

I hope you will allow me to continue to write about my exploits, as I cannot think of another who would be interested in them.

One question, if I may. While I know this will likely strike you as most peculiar, I remember that you wrote of your particular interest in Spiritism and phenomena unexplained by normal investigations. Do you know anything of the legends of vampires, and if so, do you deem them to be true or simple superstitions? I understand you are friends with Mr. Stoker, and perhaps you have discussed this topic with him. I would value your opinion on the subject, especially on the presence or absence of vampire souls. I have begun to imagine that the creatures might not be all evil. I would love to know if you have already "eliminated the impossible" and to hear about the truth that remains.

I look forward to your next novel with great anticipation and remain your greatest fan, and, if I may flatter myself, a friend.

Sincerely,

Lillian S. Holmes

When she finished her letter, George returned to her side and pressed a kiss upon her forehead. "Tonight, Lil. It's far past time that you go out to feed on your own."

"Why can't we continue as we have been doing?"

"I understand your revulsion. Through your eyes I've learned to care more about my victims than I desire. Well, between you and

Phillip, it seems like a conspiracy for complete rehabilitation." He smiled, and she knew he was doing his best to keep the moment light, but it felt anything but.

"There is no escape from this?"

"You would weaken gradually. It is one of the few things that could kill you. I am not ready to lose you just yet." He pulled her into his arms and she held him tightly, wanting nothing more than to escape to their room for another night of shared lust. "I will lead you," he promised. "And I shall show you something fun."

He pulled her by the hand and nodded to Phillip and Kitty, who watched them.

"Come, dear," Phillip said, smiling. "Let's withdraw for the evening."

Kitty bore an expression of mixed sympathy and horror, but she shook her head and followed him up the stairs.

George led Lillian through the back exit of the house, down the short path to the alley and then stopped. "Whether you believe immortality to be a curse or blessing, there is one bit of our nature that never fails to bring pleasure. Enjoy this."

Lillian stared at him in the moonlight. He wore a bit of a smile, and she thought again how handsome he was, how much he loved her. "And what is that thing?" she asked. She didn't entirely want to know, but she did want to appear strong for him.

"Why, don't you remember your pet name for your onetime foe?"

She paused before making the connection. "Ah! The Leaping Man. Truly? *I* can do the same?"

"It is a trifling, what you saw. See the broken gargoyle on the top story of that building?"

"You jest. It is five stories at least." But she saw he wasn't jesting. "How?"

"How do you walk? How do you run? You simply have the desire to do so, and then do it. It is no different. The constraints of your former life make it seem impossible, but you will overcome your fear after one try."

"I should tumble or make a scene. I cannot, George. Perhaps I could try something lower, nearer by to begin?"

"That is nearby, and low. I will go first, and you will follow me. All you must do is have the desire. Do not keep me waiting long, as I loathe being out of your company." He pressed a kiss to her lips and seemingly vanished, a whoosh slightly stirring the night air.

She looked to the building top to see him silhouetted against the moonlight, arms outstretched, waiting for her.

Lillian took a few steps to see if walking felt different to her now. Then: "Don't be stupid." She ran a few more yards, and the action gave her a desire to keep running, quickly and for a long time. This was new. She thought of Thomas's velocipede, of speeding past buildings and the joy of that, of moving without being recognized. And as she looked up again to George, she wondered what it would be like to fly.

Closing her eyes, she imagined that her velocipede could take to the air, that she could look down on the city and that it and all of its citizens had lost their power over her. Which was true. In fact—she sniffed out a laugh at herself—what was the worst that could happen? If bullets could no longer kill her, what would be the issue with this jump?

With a deep exhalation she ran a few steps and then took a giant leap, all the while looking up.

"Go there," she said aloud.

At first it felt like a fall, only one that made you go up instead of down. Within moments she found control and guided herself to land a yard away from George. Her limbs sang with energy and she hurled herself into his arms. As he lifted her from the roof and spun her around, she laughed.

"Again! I would do it again, right away!"

He laughed and set her down. "I told you so. What great times we'll be having, hopping about town together. But first—"

"What is happening there?" Across the street, in a dark corner against a building, a woman struggled as a ruffian pulled her back, one arm around her waist, the other over her mouth. She pointed so that George could find the troubling scene.

"Blazes! I will take care of him!"

But Lillian was already off, without a word to George. While she didn't experience the same enjoyment in her second flight, she felt triumphant when she landed on the ruffian with her feet, knocking his head to the cobbles. He looked up in horror as she growled and bared her teeth. Overflowing with rage, she lifted him up by the collar with one hand and landed a strong punch to his cheek with the other. The bone made a sickening crack under her fist, and she reveled in the discovery of strength pouring through her. "You will never hurt anyone again!"

She heard George calming the frantic woman behind her, urging her to run off. Still not satisfied, Lillian lifted the would-be attacker by the collar again and pounded his head to the cobbles. His eyes rolled up and he passed into unconsciousness.

"Love, be quick. He is no use to you dead."

She looked over her shoulder at George, who stared at her curiously and with a bit of admiration. She turned and leaned into her victim, exposing his neck.

"What fun," George said with a chuckle. "Another protector of Baltimore's downtrodden. Won't Phillip and Kitty be pleased."

EPILOGUE

"Who is the chit?" Marie de Bourbon snarled as she and her companion looked down on the feeding that played out far below.

"No one of consequence," Annaluisa mumbled, then winced when Marie turned and scratched her cheek with razor-sharp nails. What was the use of lying, of trying to protect George? Her efforts had already backfired badly, and having been forced to lead Marie to the Orleanses' door, she knew her usefulness to this she-devil was coming to a quick end. How much longer would she be tortured, body and spirit?

"Try answering again."

"She is a newborn, created by George only recently."

"His tastes have not improved. Does she…mean something to him?"

Anna noticed a twitch of Marie's lips, and she gulped. This would not go over well, but her resistance had worn down completely. "I am afraid to say she means a great deal to him."

"Ah." Marie quietly watched the pair below for a few moments, and Anna knew her guess had been right. Marie *had* loved George at one time.

"And she loves her maker?"

"She was dying, and he saved her."

"George saved a dying woman? The George I remember would have barely been tempted to save a dying child, even when he was mortal. I knew him then, you see."

Anna backed up a few steps; then her limbs froze, as Marie would not allow her to flee.

"This is really a boon. George can watch those he cares about suffer greatly before I feed on him." Marie turned to Anna with a broad smile. "Why not begin with you, dear?"

ABOUT THE AUTHOR

Ciar Cullen hails from Baltimore and resides in New Jersey with her husband and a few cats. She started adult life as an archaeologist, worked in publishing, and eventually became a bureaucrat at a college. She loves reading nonfiction, traveling, and—sometimes—writing. This is her fifteenth book.

LILLIAN HOLMES
AND THE LEAPING MAN

Tormented by a tragic past, Miss Lillian Holmes nonetheless found the strength to go on, to become the greatest female detective of her time. To make her uncle proud. Except…he was not truly her uncle. Sherlock was a fictional character, and Lil was less a true detective than a sheltered twenty-six year old heiress with taste for mystery…and morphine. But then she saw *him*. Leaping from her neighbor's second-story window, a beautiful stranger. With the recent murders plaguing Baltimore, here was a chance to reveal the truth.

Except, the Leaping Man was far more than he seemed. A wanton creature of darkness, an entry point to a realm of deception and evil, and to a Truth she had waited countless years to uncover, he would threaten far more than Lillian's life. He would take both her heart and soul. And she would rejoice in it.